# THE FOG DOGGIES AND ME

# THE FOG DOGGIES AND ME

### BY
## GAYLE PEARSON

### ATHENEUM 1993 NEW YORK

Maxwell Macmillan Canada
*Toronto*
Maxwell Macmillan International
*New York Oxford Singapore Sydney*

Atheneum
Macmillan Publishing Company
866 Third Avenue
New York, NY 10022

Maxwell Macmillan Canada, Inc.
1200 Eglinton Avenue East
Suite 200
Don Mills, Ontario M3C 3N1

Macmillan Publishing Company is part of the Maxwell Communication Group of Companies.

First edition
Printed in the United States of America
10 9 8 7 6 5 4 3 2 1
Book design by Kimberly M. Adlerman

**Library of Congress Cataloging-in-Publication Data**
Pearson, Gayle.
The fog doggies and me / Gayle Pearson.—1st ed.
p. cm.
Summary: Twelve-year-old Starr has as much trouble dealing with her younger sister's adoration as she does with her feelings of betrayal when her longtime best friend finds a boyfriend.
ISBN 0-689-31845-6
[1. Friendship—Fiction. 2. Sisters—Fiction. 3. Family life—Fiction.]
I. Title
PZ7.P32312Fo   1993
[Fic]—dc20                                               92-41069

**FOR KAREN,**

**A HEAVENLY LITTLE SISTER**

# THE FOG DOGGIES AND ME

# PROLOGUE

When Ivy and I were ten we tried to dig up the floor of her Uncle Paul's garage. It used to be a carriage house years ago and still had a hard dirt floor. We decided it was a likely place for buried jewels or gold coins, and as both our allowances were small, we found a pick and shovel and went at it. We hardly dented the ground. It was like trying to push a toothpick through cement.

We did find a few chunks of colored glass and a rusty key. Many future discussions revolved around this mysterious key, like why it was buried in the carriage house floor and whom it belonged to. Because we would never know, we made up a story and it went something like this:

In 1891 a sixteen-year-old girl was sent west from New York because her parents died in a flu epidemic. She came to stay with her aunt and uncle in San Francisco, but they didn't know a thing about raising children and sometimes locked her in the carriage house to teach her a lesson.

She was smart. She stole a key to the carriage house door and buried it, planning to use it to escape the next time the mean aunt and uncle locked her inside. But something happened. I said she was accidentally run over by the carriage and died. Ivy said she was rescued by her boyfriend.

"Boyfriend?" I said with surprise. I hadn't thought of that.

# CHAPTER 1

"Y ou know what I want?"

I turned to Ivy, who was sitting beside me cross-legged on a large flat rock, and said, "Is it something to wear or something to eat?"

She slapped the side of my leg and snickered. "I'm not *that* shallow. It's neither. What I want . . ." She paused to tuck in a few loose strands of her light brown hair and tighten this ratty-looking old scarf she'd had for about a hundred years.

"What I want . . . is something to *happen.*"

"Oh?" I said, raising my eyebrows. "Like what?"

"Something exciting," she beamed. "Something that's never happened to me before."

"Well, for one thing, you're turning thirteen in a few days. That's something, isn't it?"

"I know. Can you believe it!"

Actually, I almost couldn't, even though I was only six months behind her. It seemed that only last week we were nine years old, holding hands in the backseat of her parents'

Toyota wagon, as we headed off to Camp Willoughby for the very first time. We were scared to death because Vanessa Johnson told us that all the cabins had bars on the windows. We shrieked and howled and giggled hysterically all the way there, to her parents' dismay.

"Something exciting," I repeated. "Well, that could be a lot of things, Ivy. Like breaking your leg or getting an A in Spanish."

"Sí, señorita, but that's not what I had in mind."

"Well, what do you mean then?"

"I don't know. Just something exciting."

"You must have some idea."

"Maybe I won't know until it happens."

I took a deep breath, partly because what she said made me nervous, and also because I love this damp, woodsy smell, pine and eucalyptus, and whatever else was growing around us. It was a Friday afternoon in early April, and the beginning of our spring vacation. Although I enjoyed school, I was deliriously happy at the thought of a whole week off, because by this time of year we were all sick of one another. The kids, the teachers, the bus drivers, the volunteers, Pete the janitor, and even Mary Chan, who owned the little grocery store across the street.

We'd cut through the arboretum in Golden Gate Park on our way home from school. I loved this part of the park, the way it was divided into countries and climates from around the world. With a little effort I could imagine I was really in South America, New Zealand, Asia, Australia, or the New World Cloud Forest, even though I did not know what a cloud forest was. A lot of damp and dreary trees, I supposed. I preferred South America, with its nice collection of exotic-looking trees. You could stand in the densest part and imagine you were really there.

"I guess I want something exciting to happen to me too," I admitted.

"Do you? Like what?"

"Something really adventurous." I gazed at the tops of the tall, tall trees, which seemed to be swaying. "Sometimes I can see myself paddling down a dangerous river, like the Amazon, and hiking through the jungle."

"That sounds like you. I bet you got the idea from that missionary movie we saw, where the guys discovered the diamond mine."

"I wouldn't go for the diamonds. I'd go for adventure, and to study wildlife and the rain forest. You want to come?"

"No."

Her tone of voice made me steal a glance at her face, and I knew right away she was remembering her dad. I was sorry I'd mentioned paddling down a dangerous river, because he'd drowned on a rafting trip down the Colorado River when she was ten.

"I don't know why I want to do something like that." I extended my legs, letting them dangle over the side of the rock. "It must be in my blood. Mom backpacked all over Europe when she was in her twenties, you know. I'd like to go somewhere really remote, where people hardly ever go. A huge, dense rain forest full of wild beasts, and a raging, frothing river . . ." I stopped, nervously kicking the rock with the heel of my shoe, afraid I'd said the wrong thing again.

"*Frothing?*" Ivy repeated, brushing a fly from her face.

"It's such a funny word, isn't it? Do rivers froth? I thought that was like dogs foaming at the mouth."

I felt relieved, because what I'd said didn't seem to bother her this time. "Dogs and rivers. They both froth. Froth is like foam, like, you know . . ." I hesitated, because I didn't want to say white water.

She smiled. "Well, you're my best friend, Starr, but friendship has its limits. I'll take my foam on a root beer float."

I laughed, leaning forward to withdraw a small foil-wrapped package from my day pack. A look of anticipation appeared on Ivy's face as she drew herself up into a sitting position. In the beginning, when we were back in the third grade, I didn't know how funny she could be. She was so shy, so quiet and serious. I hadn't known a lot of things about her then, but I did now.

"Want a chocolate-chip cookie?" I said.

"Your dad make 'em?"

"Uh-huh."

She nodded vigorously and held out her hand. "I wonder if he'd make me a cake someday. Ma tries so hard, but that last cake was too much."

Her father had been a good cook, same as mine. I'd loved going to her birthday parties, because I knew he'd have whipped up something special in the way of a cake.

"She changes any of the ingredients she wants, like yogurt instead of sour cream, and kiwi instead of canned pineapple. It was more like a California fruit salad than a cake." She smacked her lips, a habit that sometimes annoyed me.

This time I smiled, though, because I'd already found a recipe for something called a Chocolate Heart Attack and had asked my father to help me. There would be no yogurt in this cake. We were planning a little surprise party for her birthday on Tuesday night. Although they have two of their own, my parents treat Ivy like another daughter.

"Scat!" I yelled at a small gray squirrel begging for crumbs. Then, feeling sorry for it, I relented and tossed it a small one.

"Hey, don't waste it! You got anything to drink?" Ivy yawned, rubbing a wee-size bump on the bridge of her nose. The bump was a present from me back in the third grade, when I'd accidentally smashed her nose with a soccer ball. Our PE teacher gave me a present too—my nickname: "Hammer Toe."

I passed her some juice left over from lunch.

"Thanks."

"You're welcome. Save me some." It was hot sitting on that rock in the sun. I wiped my face with the bottom of my sweatshirt and pushed my chin-length brown hair behind my ears, where it would remain for about thirty seconds. Then I folded the leftover foil into a little square and gathered the crumbs into a little pile on the rock. My mother, who writes for a computer magazine, once wrote a poem about me:

> Parents used to worry
> About kids being beatniks.
> I'm not so sorry
> To say mine's a neatnik.

I was making a conscious effort not to reach over and flick a cookie crumb from the corner of Ivy's mouth, figuring these things usually have a way of disappearing by themselves, unlike life's larger problems.

"It's like starting a new life," said Ivy.

"What is?"

"Turning thirteen."

"A *new* life? It's the *same* life, Ivy. You'll just be one day older on your birthday."

"No, I don't think so. I think it's like starting another chapter in a book. At least I hope so, because this last chapter was boring."

"Was it?" I said with surprise. I hadn't thought so and was disappointed to hear her say that. I thought we'd been having fun. "Well, you sound like you're ready for something, but I don't know what."

"I don't know either."

"I hope you don't run off and do something stupid."

"'Scuse *me?*" she said with a grimace.

"Oh well." I sighed, tossing one last crumb to about seventy squirrels gathered around the rock. "Here, you greedy little things, that's all you get. And here come the jays too. We haven't a chance."

"Oh well what? I hate those birds! Shoo! Get away from us!" She whistled shrilly, with two fingers between her teeth.

I took my hands from my ears. "Oh well, if you go off and do something stupid, I hope you learn from it."

Ivy snickered, passing me the half-empty container of juice. "Thanks. I hope you do too. Gee, you have a lot of confidence in me, don't you?"

"Well, that's what you're supposed to do when you're young, isn't it? Make mistakes and learn from them. Everyone says so. Besides . . ."

I rotated the plastic jug in my hand, not knowing how to say what I was thinking. For one thing, I felt weird because my friends all seemed in a big hurry to turn thirteen, and I wasn't. I didn't know why they were and I wasn't, and it made me feel left out, like some kind of freak. The truth was, I was happy as I was right then. I had a good life, a nice family, a best friend, and enough to eat every day. I was healthy, and happy with school too.

"Yoo hoo. I'm listening," she said, waving a hand in front of my face.

"I don't want anything to happen. I like things as they are."

"I hate to tell you this, but things always change. They can't stay the same way forever." She dusted the crumbs from her hands and stuffed a balled-up napkin into a side pocket of her jeans.

I wondered if I should say more or just drop it, then thought, oh well, she is my best friend. "I hate that, that things have to change. I mean, don't you ever worry? I'm happy now. . . ." I lifted my head and looked at her.

"Are you?" she said flatly. "That's nice. I guess I'm mostly happy too. I guess."

As I rolled up the sleeves of my sweatshirt, totally unconvinced by what she said, she suddenly blurted, "Sure I'm afraid of things changing! What if something happened to my mom?"

I hung my head, a little ashamed. "Oh, that's right," I mumbled. "I should've thought of that." I slipped my arm around her shoulder, and we sat quietly like that for a few minutes. Then she said, in a voice I could barely hear, "You know what I really want to happen? I want my dad to be here when I turn thirteen, that's all. I wish he was going to see me graduate too. I dream about him all the time. . . ."

I squeezed her shoulder, seeing an image of her father waving from behind the steering wheel of his car. He had on his green windbreaker and silver sunglasses, and his dark, wiry hair curled out from underneath a Giants cap. Letting my arm fall from her shoulder, I said, "I can't imagine what it's like, Ivy. I . . . I know it's still hard for you." I always fumbled around like that when she talked about her dad, never coming up with the right thing to say to make her feel better. "What are you doing Tuesday night? You want to come over for dinner?"

She sighed. "Sure. That'd be fun."

She leaned her head against my shoulder and said, "Promise we'll always be friends?"

"Always, I promise. Now what else do you want to do this week? It's your birthday all week. We can do something every day to celebrate, starting with a movie tomorrow. How about it?"

"Yeah, and the beach if it's nice. Maybe go shopping and read, listen to some music, watch TV, sleep in, go on a diet . . ."

"That's kind of a lot for one day, and why are you going on a diet? You're not fat. You look fine to me as you are."

"I'm fat. You know I'm fat," she whined, slapping her thighs. "So I have to go on a diet."

"You don't need to *diet*. You're fine. Trust me." I tossed the juice jug into my pack.

"Well, what would you say I am, if fat doesn't fit me?"

"I don't know." I yawned and scratched my forehead. This talk about diets didn't interest me at all. "I'd say you . . . you've got round corners."

"Oh, right. Round corners, like a baseball diamond." She wrinkled her nose in disgust. "Like . . . like elbow macaroni . . . like . . ."

"Oh, Ivy, stop it. I mean everybody's built different."

"Oh, *Starr*. You try having *round corners* for a while. See how you like it. Macaroni, I should be so lucky. Right now I feel like a big noodle, a manicotti stuffed with sausage and olives and grease. . . ."

"Gee, Ivy!"

"Well, that's how I feel. I'm telling you the truth. I'm like a big wet walking piece of starch!"

I tittered and hopped down off the rock. "How does a noodle walk? Let's see. Like this?" I paraded back and forth in front of her, wriggling side to side with a goofy look on my face.

"Starr! Stop it!"

At least I made her laugh about it. "Okay! Stop talking about being fat, then. You watch too much TV. You take those diet commercials to heart. Nobody looks like those people." I hoisted myself back up onto the rock beside her as she pulled a little green notebook and a pen from her back pocket and began writing. "You know what I'm really happy about?" I said, peering over her shoulder. "I won't have to hear Mrs. Alvarez call us the cream of the crop for a whole week."

She laughed. "Yeah, it's a relief. I've always suspected

that she said that to all her students anyway, as a way to get them to try hard. Why do you think she wears her hair down over her eyes like that? She has a nice face, but she hides it."

"I don't know. Maybe she doesn't think it's a nice face, or maybe it's just a bad habit. What're you writing?"

She finished without answering, tore the page from its little binder, and handed it to me. It said:

*Dear Hammer Toe,*

*Thanks for saying I'm not fat.*
*You're the best friend in the world.*
*What would I have done if you hadn't*
*moved here from St. Louis?*

*Love,*
*Ivy.*

"Thanks," I said. "That's nice."

"I mean it. Did we finish the cookies?"

"Yeah, we did." Right then I felt sorry for other people who didn't have a best friend like I did. In fact, I felt sorry for anyone who didn't feel as good, happy, and content as I. For once I didn't seem to have a worry in the world. Everything was going my way, and I had a week off in which to enjoy myself.

Then, as often happens when I'm feeling on top of the world, I had a sudden vision of my old Norwegian grandmother, wrapped in a shawl at her kitchen table with a cup of coffee and an apple slice, reciting her favorite proverb:

Don't let yourself be too happy today because by tomorrow you'll be miserable all over again.

I shook my head, trying to rid my mind of such gloom, wishing I were Italian, like my Aunt Sharon, whom I'm related to through marriage. She says that you can never be too happy or too rich.

So who do you believe?

CHAPTER 2

We had to go the long way out of the arboretum in order to avoid crossing this narrow footbridge over a stream. It wasn't much of a stream, but it was too much for Ivy. I tried to remember not to tease her about her fear of water. She didn't swim or go boating, and hated crossing the Golden Gate Bridge. About the only thing she did comfortably with water was drink it.

I didn't mind going out of our way. It was such a beautiful day, and the detour took us through China. All of the various species of plants and trees in the arboretum were identified by their Latin names on little signs stuck in the ground. We liked to try to pronounce them.

"*Pinus romanthus*," said Ivy, pronouncing *Pinus* to rhyme with *Venus*.

"It's *Pinus romanthus*, as in blueberry *pie*," I corrected.

"Oh, you are bad."

Some of our favorites were *Prunus vulgaris*, *Nemophila menziesii* (baby blue-eyes), and *Brugmansia volcanicola*. We thought the last one sounded like a cross between a vicious monster and a soft drink. Thus, Brugmansia became our secret nickname for Marshall Actin, a boy at school who bullied younger kids.

We stopped at a large pond near the exit to feed the ducks the stale bread we'd brought from home. Here and there people were sitting on little green benches or lying on blankets in the sun.

"Here little duckies, poor little duckies," I called. They swarmed toward us like a small brown-and-white army.

"They look awfully well fed, don't they?" I noted to Ivy as I scattered crumbs amid the wriggling and squawking.

"Very." She dipped her hand into the brown paper bag and threw out a handful. "Look, some won't eat the whole wheat, only the sourdough French."

Every time I saw these ducks I remembered Sybil, a big white duck presented to my little sister Julie and me by a neighbor on Easter, when Sybil was still a duckling. We loved her, but she was a pest. She wouldn't swim alone in her little yellow plastic swimming pool, or play by herself in the yard. She followed us everywhere. In this way she was a lot like Julie, who followed me everywhere. We finally shipped Sybil to a farm up north, where she befriended a horse and slept on the horse's back every night. We kept Julie.

As I tossed the last handful of crumbs from the bag, I noticed a man in a dark overcoat reading a newspaper on one of the benches. I had an active and powerful imagination, and I was inclined to believe that the city I lived in, San Francisco, was full of danger. When I approached the crest of a steep hill, for example, and couldn't see the bottom, I imagined there was no bottom, that it plunged to an endless, mysterious black chasm into which I could easily disappear. I was afraid that turning thirteen could be a lot like this.

"Hey, Ivy?"

"Yeah?"

"See that guy right across from us, in the dark coat?"

"Yeah?"

"He looks a little suspicious, don't you think?"

"Well, no, I wouldn't say that."

"You wouldn't? I would. It's too warm for a coat like that, and in the movies you always see undercover people meeting on little green benches."

"He's really cute, isn't he?"

"Huh?" I was surprised that she said that, as his face was hidden behind the newspaper. Ivy's imagination is not as wild as mine. In fact, sometimes it needs to be nurtured and coaxed, like a little African violet. But apparently not this time.

"Cute?" I said. "I can't see his face, but I bet it's not cute. I mean, look at that coat."

"Are you kidding? That's a great jacket. Hey, I know that guy! He's a ninth grader."

"I-vy." I was now feeling a little annoyed. "If that guy's a ninth grader, well, then . . . it's just not possible."

"Yeah it is. He's on the newspaper."

I sighed. "Ivy, he's not *on* the newspaper, he's reading it."

"Listen," she said out of the corner of her mouth, "I know who he is because last semester he sat near me in study period. He used to get nosebleeds and wear these horrible ugly socks covered with flags from around the world. He had several pairs, and they never matched his shirts. But now, gee . . ."

Glancing at her and following her gaze, I saw that we were not looking at the same person. Off to the right of the man in the overcoat, a boy in a leather jacket aimed the lens of a camera at a white egret in the middle of the pond. "Oh," I replied flatly. "That guy."

Just then a wisp of fog crawled across the bright blue sky. The trees bristled and swayed at the tops, and the little blond hairs on my arms stood straight on end. Just like there's never one duck, there's never one wisp of fog. It's a front-runner for an invasion. Good-bye, sun. So long, blue sky. Soon the agent pretending to read the newspaper and the boy who used to wear ugly socks with international flags would be swallowed up in a cool gray mist.

I shivered and stooped to pick up my pack. "I've got to get to the store for Estella."

"Wait." Ivy grabbed my elbow. "He's smiling at us. Look."

"I'm not going to look at him if he's smiling at us!" But I did. I glanced up at him quickly, and then at the ground. He was smiling at us, and ever so slowly edging his way around the pond.

"What's he photographing?" she asked me. "It's not us, is it?" She yanked off the ratty scarf and shook her head to fluff up her hair.

"No. But if you stand on one leg and dunk your head in the water, he might."

"Oh, *Starr*." She giggled.

I dug my hands into my pockets, then took them out and rolled down the sleeves of my sweatshirt. Just seeing those puffs roll across the sky made me chilly. My tolerance for fog is about equal to my tolerance for Julie. I can handle them both for about an hour, as a way to break up the day. I have felt more kindly toward fog, however, since my father told me about an article he recently read in a magazine. It said that scientists, using powerful microscopes, have discovered that fog is actually made up of microscopic dogs. Thus, the similarity between the words *fog* and *dog*.

"I just can't believe it's the same boy." Ivy glanced at him and looked away, glanced at him and looked away. He was doing the same thing. "But it is, and he's heading this way. What should we do?"

I couldn't believe it was the same *day*. I was starting to freeze.

She squeezed my elbow hard. "Ouch! That hurt!" I cried. So much for my story about a secret agent. It was a silly idea anyway, I thought. I was too old for stuff like that. "He's just trying to get the egret from another angle, Ivy. Don't get so . . . so worked up about nothing. I mean, gee. He might be cuter now, but why don't you check out his socks before you get carried away?"

"I can't do that unless he's sitting down. And we're not in study together." She seemed a bit hysterical. I felt a little sorry for her.

"Maybe if we go sit on that bench, he'll join us. Then we can both check out his socks. We can vote on them. It must be unanimous."

She started giggling and couldn't seem to stop. That got me going and we both stood there cackling over nothing, like idiots. Then she pulled the green notebook from her back pocket and started writing.

"What are you doing? Hoping he'll think you're a writer and ask you to join the newspaper?"

"Ha! No, I'm reminding myself to get some nice barrettes. I hate this old scarf." She flipped the notebook shut and slipped the scarf and the notebook back into her pocket. As she regained her composure, I made a mental note about ideas for her birthday present.

"Do you think he's cute or what?" she asked.

"What?"

"I said do you think he's cute or *what?*"

"I don't know."

"You must have an opinion."

"I do. I like his jacket."

"That's not helpful."

"Well, it's hard to see well from here. And the fog's rolling in."

"What does *that* have to do with it?"

"I want to go! I don't want to look at him anymore!"

"Oh, all right, Starr."

"You should talk about his socks," I said.

"What do you mean?"

"That old scarf of yours has little balloons all over it. Isn't that what they are? Let's see!" I yanked it from her back pocket and held it up to examine. "See, it looks like wrapping paper!"

We started laughing again, and when we were all worn out, Ivy said, "Oh, let's just go. I'm afraid he'll come over, and I won't know what to say."

"Ask him who does his shopping."

She sputtered into another fit of laughter.

"Poor Ivy," I said. "Here's your scarf."

"You . . . you keep it. I don't ever want to *see* it again."

"Fine with me. Poor little orphan scarf." I folded it in half, corner to corner, put it on my head, and tied it under my chin. "How do I look?"

She was laughing again and could hardly talk. "You . . . you look like your grandmother."

"Aha! A babushka, like Grandma Anna. I, however, am not afraid to be happy!"

I was, however, getting colder. We hurried from the arboretum as the fog doggies raced across the sky in swirling gobs of gray. It was amazing how fast that sun could disappear.

CHAPTER 3

Something moist and sticky was leaking through the bottom of the bag, probably the mocha almond fudge ice cream. I slipped the key into the lock, shoved the iron gate open, inserted another key into the outside door, and ran up the dirty wooden staircase.

Estella lived on the third floor of a three-story building not far from the park. I had my own keys because it saved her a trip to the buzzer. She had bad arthritis in her legs.

I got this job because my mother's friend's daughter couldn't do it any longer. Estella was a shut-in and had nobody. Her son lived in L.A. Her daughters were back in Guatemala, which sounds like "What-a-mala" when you say it in Spanish. At first I loved it, my first real paid job outside of baby-sitting. It seemed like an adventure. After a while, though, the newness wore off and it wasn't as much fun.

I knocked twice to let her know I was here, then inserted the third key into the door to her apartment and shoved it open with my knee.

"The Giants are ahead, three to one in the fifth." She was sitting in her chair in front of the TV. She always told me the score, as though I'd dropped by to watch the ball game.

"Great. I'll put these things away. The ice cream's melting."

She smiled broadly, revealing a broken front tooth and a small gap where a tooth once had been. Her skin was the color of a copper kettle, her face a web of fine, deep lines. "Ice cream? Oh, you're such a nice little girl."

I blushed as I emptied my backpack on the kitchen counter, embarrassed by the compliment. After I put away the cans of beans and soup, the bananas, milk, rice, TV dinners, ice cream, and Pepsi-Cola, I wandered back into the living room. I was already sniffling from the smell of Jungle Gardenia, her favorite cologne, and I didn't feel much like hanging around on my first day of vacation. But I knew she was lonely.

I sat down on the worn brown sofa next to Estella's chair, where she sat wrapped in her colorful shawl and bright wool blanket. "I think I forgot something," I said, "but I don't know what."

She smiled. Maybe she was hoping I had, so I'd have to come back. "You got Pepsi?" she asked.

"Yep."

"You got beans?"

"Yep."

"You got rice?"

"Yep."

"I'm hungry."

I swiveled to see Estella's parrot, Isabel, hanging by her toes from a lampshade. "I'm hungry. Make me a sandwich," she squawked.

"Hi, Isabel," I said.

"I'm hungry. Make me a sandwich." She swung side to side. This made me dizzy.

"Say hi and stop showing off," said Estella.

"Hi, and make me a sandwich," said Isabel.

Estella shook her head sternly but couldn't help smiling. "What a character. It's the fifth inning. Do you want a Pepsi-Cola?"

I shook my head. "No, thanks." A warm Pepsi stood on the floor beside Estella's chair. She was always sipping warm Pepsi, saying that's how she drank it in Guatemala.

I rubbed my nose and sniffed. The Jungle Gardenia, once promoted by a game-show host, was everywhere in the apartment.

"This umpire's a bum."

"Yeah?" I tried to stifle a yawn, but it came out anyway. It was hot in there. Then Isabel opened her little beak in a wide mimic yawn. *"Aaaaaahhhh."* It was eerie. She sounded just like me.

"Look at that! See! He say 'strike' for *ball* and 'ball' for *strike* and gets batter all mixed up. C'mon, Waddell, be a hitter."

I turned to look out the window, but the blinds were drawn and covered with dust. I rubbed my nose again.

She sipped from her can of Pepsi and lowered it to the floor. "School is good?"

"Yeah. But over for a week. Spring vacation."

"You want to come watch baseball?" She smiled in anticipation. I gazed at the black space between her teeth.

"Uh," I began, not knowing how to say no.

"No, you're busy. You're young and pretty. You have friends. And a boyfriend?" Her whole face lit up and her eyes danced with mischief.

I pretended to laugh a little, shaking my head. But it always annoyed me when adults asked these probing questions about my personal life. I didn't have a boyfriend and didn't want one. The girls who had them worried about them. Would so-and-so steal her boyfriend? Would they make it through the summer or run out of gas? It was a little like owning a car. You could trade in an old model for a new one, or simply swap with your friends.

I didn't hate boys. I just didn't need one now. And I got tired of their shoving and pushing and clumping around with heavy feet and big hands, their loud showing off. I'd seen Ivy's brother Troy down a quart of milk standing in front of the open refrigerator, put the empty carton back inside, then say, "Ma always says to leave things where you find them."

I liked the boys who were a little different, like Robby Palmer. He was quiet, planned to be a vet or zoologist. But he often wore animal T-shirts to school, like the one with the front of the horse on the front of his shirt and its behind on his back. I didn't find that particularly attractive.

"Neither Ivy nor I plan to have boyfriends for quite a while," I told her. "We're not in a hurry." I thought briefly of the boy at the pond and then quickly forgot him.

"Nah," Estella agreed. "You don't need a boyfriend.

You're just a girl. You don't want to get married yet." Up went the can of Pepsi, and down again.

*Married,* I said to myself. Who was talking about *marriage?* I felt myself turn a little red. "Well . . ." I began inching forward on the sofa. Maybe it was time to get going.

"My cousin Felix"—she grinned, sticking her tongue where her tooth should've been—"was my first boyfriend."

"Really?" I ran through my list of boy cousins. No way.

"Sure! All my cousins were handsome and strong. Felix drove a taxi so the *turistas* could come to buy blankets. Our village was up in the mountains. Sometimes I rode with him in his taxi. He held my hand and drove with his other hand. He was thirteen and I was eleven. He liked to kiss."

I jumped as Isabel burst across the room. "Kiss me!" she squawked, landing on Estella's shoulder. "Kiss me!" Estella turned, planting a noisy kiss on her beak. Then Isabel made this loud kissing sound, a long, low-sounding smack.

"How does she do that?" I asked.

"It's from TV. She's a good listener." She leaned closer to me and whispered, "I don't put on 'Wheel of Fortune,' or she says, 'I'd like to buy an *E* please, I'd like an *R* please,' all night long. She even whistles at the girl."

"Does she solve the puzzles?"

"No," laughed Estella. "You're not that smart, are you, Izzy?"

Isabel glared straight ahead with her black beady eyes, her toes dug into the shawl on Estella's shoulder. A dog barked somewhere in the building. Isabel began barking too. *"Woof argh argh. Woof argh argh."*

"You should take her with you. Then I could have some

peace," complained Estella, but she was smiling. I knew she didn't mean it. She once told me how Isabel liked to curl up next to her on her pillow at night. She would pull her hair and whistle. Estella had whistled and pulled at a strand of black hair to show me.

I stood and snapped my fingers. "Here, Lassie, here, Lassie," I called. "C'mon home with me."

"*Woof woof argh argh. Woof woof argh argh.*"

"I think she likes *you*, Estella."

"You going?"

"Yes. What happened to Felix?"

"He became a tuba player for the symphony in Mexico City. All that kissing was good practice. Right, Izzy?" She grinned as Isabel did a little jig on her shoulder, excited from all the attention.

"She's better than me," I admitted. "I'm a terrible dancer."

"Me too." Estella pointed to her feet, wrapped in ankle supports. I only laughed because she did.

"This pitcher fat like a burrito. How can he throw the ball?"

"Burrito," I said, slapping my forehead. "I forgot the tortillas."

Estella smiled. "Oh, that's okay. Next time."

I knew she ate tortillas every day. So I apologized and promised to bring some by the next day.

"Yeah?" said Estella. She looked really happy.

As I descended the stairs two at a time the neighbor's dog began barking like crazy, and I could hear Isabel too. "*Woof, woof, argh, argh.*" I smiled, thinking, cute personality, then realized it was something my grandmother would say about one of my friends: "Nice girl, cute personality."

My grandmother has lived alone since my grandfather died, but she doesn't seem lonely. She has her whole family living nearby. As I skipped down the last few stairs, and Isabel's "barking" grew fainter, I wondered what it would be like to have a bird as your only companion.

# CHAPTER 4

When I first awoke on Saturday morning, I readied myself in the usual way for action: Throw off the covers, plant two feet on the floor, stumble to the bathroom. Then I remembered the day, sighed with relief, rolled onto my right side, stretched, and yawned, gloating over the thought of a week's vacation. It was Saturday morning, and I could see the whole week stretching before me like a blank sheet of paper. Yawning again, I drew my knees to my chest and curled up into a happy little ball. Until I heard a little something. . . .

Nibble nibble . . . crunch crunch . . .

I was not yet ready to face daylight, but, curious, I opened one eye.

"Noooo," I groaned. The little something was a rat named Julie, perched on the end of my bed, chomping on a hunk of chocolate.

"Off my bed, please. I'm sleeping." I squeezed my eyes shut and rolled over, determined to go back to sleep, or at least to lie there awhile in peace.

Nibble nibble . . . crunch . . . crunch . . . "Rachel said she was inviting eight kids to her party and I might be one of them. It was between me and Tanis Shepherd. I hope it's me."

I turned over again and cocked another eye open. "What are you eating?"

She was smiling, happy that I was now paying attention. "It's a Goo Goo Supreme. You want one?"

"No. Does Mom know you're eating junk before breakfast?"

"This is breakfast."

"Then eat it at the table. And get the crumbs off my bed." I rolled over again, folding the pillow around my head. Goo Goo Supreme? I wondered, slipping a hand under my pajama top to get at an itch on my back. What on earth was a Goo Goo Supreme? Baby food? A singing group? A group of baby singers?

The pillow did not drown her crunching and smacking, only muffled it, as though I were under water, and a big fish was snacking right above me. I raised myself onto my elbows and glared at her. "If you spill chocolate on my bed . . . !"

Her hand fluttered across the bedspread, swishing crumbs this way and that. "All the kids invited will get a beauty treatment. You know, instead of going for pizza. Facial or nails. You have to choose. I'll get my nails done if I'm picked."

"Could you please get that thing out of here!"

"You want one? I have a lot."

"No. What do you mean, 'a lot'?"

"I bought four pounds for twenty dollars."

I sat all the way up and shoved the pillow between my back and the wall. "You didn't spend all of your birthday money on junk, did you? I sure hope not, Julie."

"Yes, I did. They were having a sale."

"*Who* was having a sale?"

"This catalog place in Tennessee. Goo Goo Supremes. You can't get them here. Chocolate, pecans, caramel, marshmallow . . . mmm. Here, try it." She leaned forward, thrusting the thing in my face.

"*No! Keep it away from me!* Do Mom and Dad know you spent all that money on *junk?*"

"Next time I'm ordering rock candy and Fireballs."

Maybe she was adopted. Maybe her real mother ate Goo Goos in Tennessee. I slid out of bed and went for my robe in the closet. This was the first day of vacation, and I wasn't going to let it slip through my hands watching my little sister eat Goo Goos.

I stopped by the laundry room on my way down the hallway. I was looking for my favorite sweatshirt, a present from my dad. It said, *Veni, Vidi, Vici* in Latin on the front (sounds like Weenie, Weedie, Weaky). On the back it said, I Came, I Saw, I Conquered. I *always* wore it to soccer practice. It was not in the hamper. It was not on the back of the sofa, where I was sure I'd left it the night before.

"Hmph," I muttered. I stepped back into the hallway and swung around the corner into my room. Magically, Julie appeared in the doorway.

"I wish they would grow faster, though."

Still thinking about my sweatshirt, I turned to look at her. "What?"

"My nails." She held up her hand.

I felt my patience slipping away, replaced by an urge to plunge her hand into a bag of fertilizer.

"Tanis is the one who made up the poems about everyone in our class:

> "'Wanda Wanda
> Ride my Honda.
> Will Will
> Took a spill.
> Mario Mario
> Ate an Oreo.
> Juan Juan
> Please be gone.
> Courtney Courtney
> Has a pork knee.'

"Some are better than others," added Julie. "I could do some, too, if I wanted:

> "Dwight Dwight
> Out like a light."

I took a deep breath and let it out slowly. Lucky that her voice was like wallpaper. After a while you didn't notice. Most nine-year-olds despise their older sisters, but mine adored me, no matter what I did. Anywhere in the house I went she was at my heels, yapping away like a nervous Chihuahua, or creeping up behind me like a little wisp of fog. Fog dog. Dog fog. Things were not what they seemed.

"Where's my soccer shirt, Julie? I left it on the sofa."

She was bouncing her skinny butt up against my door-jamb. *Bam. Bam. Bam.* "What shirt?" she asked innocently. "I don't know what happened to your shirt. Is it the one in Latin?"

"C'mon, Julie. I don't have time for this. I'm running late already."

"I don't know about any shirt, Starr. Sorry." She shrugged, her hands clasped behind her. *Bam. Bam. Bam.*

"All right. I'll wear something else. It doesn't matter that much. Just don't ask for any special favors this week. I'm going to be very busy." I dug around the bottom drawer of my dresser, finally yanking a plain red sweatshirt from the heap. I made a mental note to remember to straighten up later. It wasn't like me to be so messy.

"Busy doing what?"

"Going to the movies, shopping, going out for ice cream." I said the last thing just for spite, because ice cream and candy were the dearest things to her heart. "You ought to remember that next time you think of swiping something of mine."

"Maybe Mom borrowed it. Or maybe the cat ran off with it. Yeah, I bet Thelma took it. I bet that's what happened."

We didn't have a cat. We couldn't, because of Mom's allergies. I didn't know who Thelma was.

"Oh, Julie, stop it! And stop twisting your hair like that."

She stopped banging the doorjamb with her butt. Now she'd wound a long wad of hair around her hand and wrapped it around her face, like some exotic dancer. Her hair was the only thing of hers that I envied. It was the color of Swiss cheese, while mine was the color of weak tea.

"Starr?"

"*What*, Julie?" I pulled the sweatshirt down over my head and got down on all fours to look under my bed for shoes.

"*Carin*, not Julie. I always have to remind you."

Julie does not like her name. She says it makes her sound like an old woman. I say what about *Romeo and Juliet*— Juliet was only fourteen. She says she didn't know any boys named Romeo, and anyway it wasn't called *Romeo and Julie*. She wants everyone to call her Carin. Not Karen but Ca-rin. Ca-rin, as in *ca*-lamity, and *ca*-tastrophe.

"Okay, Ca-rin, what is it this time?" I sneezed, *achoo*, as I reached for a shoe amid a cluster of dustballs.

"If I find your shirt could we do something after your practice? Go to the park or something like that?"

"I was just there yesterday. If you find my sweatshirt I won't give your Barbie doll a crew cut. How's that?"

She looked sulky, slumped against the doorjamb, eating her hair. I had this theory about Julie, about something that happened three years ago, when she was six and out shopping with Mom at the Emporium on Market Street. She got lost in the lingerie department. I was convinced that standing forlornly for fifteen minutes, all by herself among the racks of bras and slips, nightgowns and lacy underthings had affected her emotional development. Maybe the world no longer seemed safe. To this day she hates bras and lacy underthings and says she'll never wear them. No telling what would've happened had she been lost in the shoe department, or coats.

I was dressed and ready to go, poking around in my jacket pocket for change for a soda after practice. "I can't go to the park anyway, even if I wanted to. I'm going to the movies." I hesitated for just a second, then, in a whiny voice, said, "Can I go?" My timing was perfect.

Our little duet made her smile. I was mad at her but didn't have the heart to say, "Find a friend your own age." She didn't have a friend, not a really good one. She played with some kids in the neighborhood and liked a few girls at school. But she didn't have a friend like I had Ivy. I wished that she did. But I didn't want it to be me.

"Starr?"

"What?"

"Can I come watch you play?"

"No, you'd be bored. You can come to a game later on." I took a deep breath and exhaled slowly. She always, *always* asked if she could come watch me play.

"Could you pick up some Golden Schoolboy cookies on your way home? I think we're out." She abruptly turned and headed down the hallway, which made her request seem like an order.

"How many boxes?" I yelled sarcastically.

"Seven, no, eight!"

Such a nervy little twit, I thought, and laughed to myself. No wonder she didn't have a friend.

The phone rang and Julie answered it. "For you!"

It was Ivy. "Guess what?" she said.

"What?"

"You just won't believe it."

"*What?*"

"Guess who called me?"

"Um, Ivy, like I'm really running late."

"Oh. Well, you know my little green notebook?" she said a little breathlessly.

"Yeah?"

"It must've fallen out of my pocket when we were fooling around at the pond. Guess who found it?"

"Not the guy with the ugly socks." I chuckled.

"Yep. I forgot to tell you his name's Stephen Salazar. I didn't care that much about the notebook, but what could I say? My phone number was in it. I couldn't tell him to throw it away. I just hope he hasn't read anything. I can't even remember everything I wrote in there. Oh, God, I hope he hasn't read it. I'm so embarrassed I could die. He's coming by any second. What should I say?"

"Say thank you. Ask him who buys his clothes."

"Oh, Starr," she wailed. "What time is the movie?"

"Two-thirty. I'll come by at two o'clock." Shaking my head, I set the receiver back in the phone's cradle.

"Starr, does Ivy have a boyfriend?"

"No. Why would you even say something like that?"

"Well, you guys are getting to that age."

"Age? What age?"

"You know." She stepped around the corner into the kitchen, grinning foolishly, draped in my Latin sweatshirt.

"Oh, look, it's Miss Weaky, wearing my sweatshirt," I snipped.

Julie stuck out her tongue.

I said, "Julie, Julie, you're unruly."

"Oh, that's good!" she exclaimed. "Could you write some poems for me so I get invited to the party?"

"Sure. I can write you something. Here's a little sample:

*"The squirt in my shirt*
*Is gonna get hurt.*

"How's that?"

She took a step backward, then stuck out her tongue and ran down the hallway.

I shook my head, more than slightly disgusted. But I was still basically in a good mood. Jiggling the change in my pocket, I headed off to practice.

# CHAPTER 5

The note on my pillow, scribbled on a piece of blue toilet paper, said:

*Dear Starr:*

*Please meet me at the water fountain in the park at 12:45 sharp. Don't forget. I'll be wating.*

*Love,*
*Carin*

I grabbed the note, crumpled it up, and charged across the hall to the bathroom, where I flushed it down the toilet with a considerable amount of annoyance. My team had had a hard practice and I was tired. I wanted to read and relax before I went to the movie with Ivy, not scramble off to the park to meet Julie. *Twelve forty-five sharp,* I seethed, with a quick glance at the bathroom mirror. What nerve.

She was not even permitted to go to the park alone.

This was a city park, an *urban* park, where weird people might shoot up drugs in the bushes.

I strode down the hall to make a sandwich, noting the time as I entered the kitchen. It was 11:45 A.M.

"Hi, Ma. I get any calls?" I opened the refrigerator door, peering inside for good sandwich material.

She glanced up from several neat piles of paperwork fanned across the kitchen table.

"Agnes Pimpledorf."

"Oh, good. She finally called me back." I smiled in spite of myself. Making up names was a minor little hobby of my mom's. Perhaps she should have had more children, or written novels instead of articles on computers.

I was lucky, really, to be named Starr after Ringo Starr of the Beatles, and glad my parents were not fans of the Grateful Dead. Once, sorting through my parents' old record collection, I knew just how lucky I was. They had albums and tapes by the Electric Prunes, Iron Butterfly, Country Joe and the Fish, Frank Zappa and the Mothers of Invention, the Guess Who, Hot Tuna, Harpers Bizarre, the Moody Blues, Pink Floyd, Moby Grape, and so on. I could've been Tuna, or Zappa, or Blue.

Parents have a lot of power, labeling you for a lifetime. Your mom or dad could say, "What do you want for lunch, tuna?" Or they could say, "What do you want for lunch, Tuna?"

I pulled out a bowl of tuna fish and took the bread down off the top of the refrigerator.

"You find something to eat? You want me to make you a sandwich?"

"No, thanks. I'll do it." As I took two pieces of whole wheat bread from the loaf and set it back on the refrigerator, I made a mental note to pick up Estella's tortillas on the way home from the movie. Then I started picking the little green onions from the bowl of tuna with a fork.

"Still going to the movies?"

"Yep."

"What's this about Ivy's new boyfriend?"

"Boyfriend?" I shook my head, smiling. "There's no boyfriend. A weird guy we saw at the park found something she lost. He's bringing it over. That's all."

"That's nice of him. How weird? He's not a psycho killer, is he?" *Clunk* went her tea mug on the kitchen table.

"No. He's a psycho dresser. Actually he had on a nice jacket, but we couldn't see much else, particularly his socks."

"Ha!" laughed my mother, removing her glasses. "Is that how you judge a guy's potential these days? By his socks?"

"Well, I've never thought about it before. But Ivy says this guy used to wear ugly socks at school."

"That's nothing. When I was in high school I went out with this guy who slept with his basketball."

"You're kidding!" I looked up from the growing mound of green onions. "Why'd he do that?"

"I think for good luck."

"I'm glad you didn't marry him."

"We didn't go out for very long. He really loved basketball."

"How come you went out with Dad?"

"He asked me, and I didn't have anything to do that

night. Then when he talked about his secret recipe for peanut butter fudge on our very first date, I thought, gee, maybe I would like to try some, and one thing led to another." She smiled, twirling a pencil between two fingers.

I'd heard this story before, but that was all right. She liked to tell it, and I didn't mind hearing it again. I yanked opened the refrigerator and pulled out the vegetable bin for two pieces of lettuce. I would put the tuna on the lettuce and not directly on the bread. This kept the bread from getting mushy. I would put some mayonnaise on the bread, however, but just a quarter teaspoon per slice.

"Oh, Ivy can come on Tuesday. I didn't say it was for her birthday, but she'll probably figure it out. I have to think of something to get her."

"Good. I'm glad she can come, and I'm glad your father will do his usual baking. See how handy that sort of thing comes in?"

"Yeah, I'll remember that, Ma. Actually, we're baking a cake together."

"Oh, that's nice. Want to shop with me on Monday night?"

"Sure." I spread mayonnaise right up to the crust on both sides of each slice—moist, but not mushy. Then I topped each slice with a piece of lettuce, and reached for the bag of potato chips.

"Is the psycho dresser actually coming to her house?"

"I guess so. I wouldn't want him to come to mine."

"Thank you, God, for a sensible daughter. No reason to hurry with stuff like that anyway. I wouldn't trade my twenties for anything."

"But you didn't have *me*, Mom."

"No, but I have you *now*," she said, smiling.

I slapped the tuna on the lettuce, wondering why she was telling me not to hurry. I wasn't in a hurry. I then slid the sandwich off the cutting board and onto a plate. I scooped up the little mound of green onions and dropped them back into the bowl of tuna salad.

"So what are you up to now? Want to come with your dad and me to buy weed killer?"

"No, thanks, Ma. I'm in the middle of a good book, so I'm going to read while I eat." I grabbed the plate and was on my way out of the kitchen, thinking about how my parents were still gaga for each other. Not all the time, but a lot of it. They'd be happy buying weed killer together.

"Your dad and I are going to weed and reap, and you're going to read and weep."

I chuckled, turning to add, "I thought it was an organic garden."

"It is organic. We'll buy a natural weed killer."

"You mean, like little bugs or what?"

"I hope not. Let me know where you're going if you go out. Hey, where's your sister?"

"I don't know. She's meeting me at the park in about an hour."

"An *hour*?" But where is she now?"

I shrugged. "Don't know, Mom." This was as much as snitching, but with no role models at home, I have never been a good liar.

"If she went by herself she's in for big trouble."

"Yeah, well, I just wish she'd make some friends of her own. Know what I mean?"

"Yes," she sighed sadly. "Well, you better eat and go get her."

I turned and headed down the hallway toward my room, almost wishing I'd lied about Julie. The truth was I didn't want to get her into trouble. I also didn't want anything bad to happen to her at the park, so I started nibbling on the sandwich before I even got to my room.

I spun through the silver turnstile into the arboretum, which looked to be a lot more crowded than the day before. I was torn between hurrying to save Julie from imagined drug dealers and kidnappers, and going real slow so she'd have to sit and wait for me awhile. I did not want her to think for a minute that she could order me around like that.

I walked briskly past the little store and nature library, past the trees with bright purple flowers, past the people eating brown-bag lunches on little green benches. The sun was warm on my back as I headed through a field of white clover. I suddenly felt happy. Maybe it was the sun, maybe it was the green field and everything blooming, or maybe it was the start of my spring vacation.

I checked my watch and cut off to the left, past a string of small ponds. In the first pond I saw a reflection of a pink-blossomed tree so clear and brilliant I nearly gasped. Something melted inside me, and I thought, Oh, that silly Julie! Oh, the month of April!

In the second pond I saw a snowy white egret on legs like stilts, striding between lily pads. I stopped when it did, watching as it rounded its neck and stared down into the water. I was amazed when it nabbed a fish but didn't stay to watch the poor thing get eaten.

At the third pond I saw an officer on horseback come clomping down the path and I wondered if something had happened. I took off running down the path toward the fountain.

I really started to worry when I got to the fountain, because Julie wasn't there. Then I saw driven into the ground with a stick a small piece of paper. I sighed, bending to pull it up. It said:

*Dear Miss Veni, Vedi, Vici,*

*I am in Southwetern Astralia. By Pinus sylvestris. Please don't be lat. I'm hungry. I hope you brought the cookies.*

*Love,*
*Carin*

I could see what she was up to. I used to come home from the park and try to tell her what a funny time Ivy and I'd had trying to pronounce the Latin names for flowers and trees. It never sounded as funny at home, but it still made her jealous. Whenever she and I went to the park she'd try to make me laugh by pronouncing the Latin names in a funny way, but it was never as funny with her. I tried, though. Once I asked her if she'd rather be *Nemophila maculata*, or baby blue-eyes. She said baby blue-eyes, but it was the wrong answer, so neither of us laughed. She did have baby blue eyes, though, something else I envied.

Now I was not in such a good mood. I glanced at my

watch again—it was 12:55 right on the nose—then stood for a moment chewing on a fingernail as I pondered the quickest route to "Southwetern Astralia." Should I cross this footbridge off to my left, or head through this grove of fir trees to my right? Beneath my feet the wood chips were damp and heavy-scented. Over my head the redwood trees towered like mighty giants. A hummingbird fed from a vivid orange flower.

"Starr!"

I raised my head, glad that Julie had returned to the fountain. But it was not Julie. I blinked several times in the bright sunlight. It was Ivy, and she was not alone. Beside her stood the psycho dresser, and then *click*. I blinked again as he lowered his camera.

"Gotcha," he said.

# CHAPTER 6

S tarr!"

My mouth fell open in surprise as Ivy rushed to my side, the psycho dresser right on her heels.

"Starr, this is Stephen!" She was out of breath and her face was flushed. She didn't quite look like herself.

"Hi." I smiled, glancing from her to him and back to her again, but suddenly I felt stiff, awkward, and tongue-tied.

"I got my notebook back. He brought it over." She nodded toward Stephen.

"Good. That's nice." I smiled at Stephen. "So . . ."

"How was practice?" Ivy grinned at me, stabbing the ground with the toe of her little white tennis shoe.

"Oh fine. It was about the same. . . ." I studied her, tilting my head first to one side and then the other. She seemed different. Why was she grinning and kicking the ground like that? Perhaps she was trying to send me a message, and if so, then what? It wasn't really true that practice had been the same as always, but I knew I'd feel funny talking about personal things in front of somebody I didn't

45

know. Later, after the movie, I would give her a step-by-step account of how our coach, while running backward down the field, tripped over a dog and wrenched her back.

"We call Starr 'Hammer Toe.' She's one of the best players on the team." She began to rub the wee little bump on her nose, as she often did when anxious or excited.

I blushed and tried to give Ivy a look. We didn't know this boy, not really, and I didn't want him to know I had a nickname. It was too personal.

"Hammertoes are genetic," said Stephen, smiling in a condescending way as he looked at my feet. "Do you really have one?"

"Huh?" I looked down at my feet too, feeling the color creep up my neck.

"The first joint of the toe is permanently bent downward, like a claw."

Something caught in my throat. I couldn't answer him. I just kept looking at my feet.

"No, you don't have one of those, do you?" asked Ivy. "We just made it up."

"Right," I blurted. "It was made up. My feet are . . . normal."

"That's good, because it would only get worse with age," said Stephen. "You'd have to have special shoes."

"Oh, goodness," said Ivy.

I lifted my head to look at her. I'd never heard her say that before. My grandmother said that a lot. "Oh, goodness." She used to say "Oh, goodness" and rub her hammertoe. Perhaps, if it was genetic, I would have one of my own someday too. It certainly was not something to look forward to, but I shrugged, deciding not to worry about it now. Instead, I tried to think of something to say to change the subject. But Stephen beat me to it.

"So you're one of the best players. That's genetic too," said Stephen. "Is that why they call you Starr?"

He said this in a mocking sort of way, and it did not please me. I shook my head. I didn't know why he was prodding into my personal life when he didn't know me, but I didn't like that either. I certainly wouldn't tell him I was named after Ringo Starr of the Beatles. This would give him information about my parents, who were out there somewhere innocently buying organic weed killer.

"She's just glad her name isn't Pupil, or Bright," chuckled Ivy.

Stephen chuckled too. It made me feel they were ganging up on me, but I smiled just a little, because I was raised to be polite, and this boy was the photographer for the *Clarion*. I also tried to catch Ivy's eye without his noticing. But she wasn't looking at me. She was looking at him, so I did too, and decided he was nothing special. Average height and build, decent face, okay eyes, and boring haircut. But he had on a cute T-shirt. It said: Don's Bait Shop and Sushi Bar, and in smaller letters, Today's Bait Is Tomorrow's Plate. This disappointed me. I wondered if I could still think of him as the psycho dresser and decided I could. One T-shirt did not a normal dresser make.

"Take a look at that hummingbird, just for example," said Stephen.

It looked like the same orange hummingbird I'd seen earlier, but I didn't know why we were looking at it now.

"Yeah," I replied, "it's got tiny little hammertoes." Stephen didn't laugh, but Ivy and I did. I was glad I'd said something funny. I felt like she was on my side again.

"We were talking about dinosaurs before you got here," she explained. "Some were built more like lizards, and others like birds."

"Oh," I replied flatly.

"And genetics," said Stephen. "We were talking about genetics, because genetics is everything. Even the little hummingbird is a direct descendant of the dinosaur. You might not think that, but it's true."

"I know—," I began to say.

"Take a look at the turkey."

I looked around but didn't see one.

"It's got the same physiological stamp as the dinosaur. So does the vulture, and more than eight thousand species of birds. Same air-cooling system in the chambers of the brain."

It was like talking to a magazine. I looked at Ivy, ready to engage in a conspiratorial smile. But she was entranced. She was mesmerized.

"It's amazing, how catastrophic changes can force mutations," he added.

I looked at Ivy again. Her eyes had glazed over. I looked at his lips, constantly moving.

Now I really wanted to see this guy's socks, because I thought if they were really ugly, I'd feel a lot better. But he was wearing green high-tops, and I couldn't see them.

"So you're a good player," said Stephen.

"She's a lot better than me," Ivy conceded, shaking her head. "I don't play much anymore."

That was the first time I'd heard her say she was inferior to me in anything. "I don't know," I said. "You've got some pretty good moves, as I recall."

"Does she? What *kind* of moves?"

"*Stephen!*"

I'd never heard her screech like that before, not in all of our years of friendship. She was also swaying side to side, and it made me a little dizzy, like watching Isabel hang from a lampshade.

Suddenly I remembered why I was here and looked at my watch. It was now one o'clock and I was late. I quickly checked the area around the fountain to make sure Julie hadn't come back looking for me.

"Looking for someone?" asked Stephen. He pointed his camera right at me.

It wasn't his business, so I shrugged instead of answering. The truth was, I didn't want to say I was meeting my little sister. I was also afraid that any second she might charge out of the bushes with a Goo Goo in her hand. I smiled, in case he took the picture.

"She's always looking around like that," said Ivy, my very best friend in the world. "It's part of her training. She's going to be an archaeologist, or some sort of explorer. Aren't you, Starr?"

I glared at her, right into her gray-gold eyeballs, and gulped. Whatever I'd said to Ivy about my hopes and dreams and plans, I never expected she'd offer them up to some boy I didn't know as a tidbit of conversation.

"Well, if you plan to be an explorer," said Stephen, lowering his camera to make a point, "I hope you like to fly."

What was that supposed to mean? I wondered, thinking

he was awfully generous with his opinions. "Why?" I asked flatly.

"Because, simply put, that is the future. With technology advancing at its rapid pace, exploration on earth soon will be complete. You'll have to be an astronaut, or whatever we'll call them by then."

"Yeah," said Ivy, nodding vigorously. "That's right."

I guessed she would have agreed with him if he'd said I'd have to explore the inside of a tomato. He was wrong, for one thing. Most ocean areas had yet to be explored. I pressed my lips together and kicked a stone, wishing it were something bigger. I suddenly felt very annoyed.

"Watch out for Hammer Toe," said Stephen. "She's just warming up."

"There are the remains of whole civilizations still buried under the ground," I declared, unclenching my teeth. "That's really what I'm interested in."

Ivy's feet were a whirlwind of action. Up on her toes and down, twist to the left and then to the right. One toe stabbed the ground like a bull's hoof and then the other. I half expected her to start snorting.

"Well, archaeology. That's really a different subject," said Stephen.

Ivy laughed, then snorted and covered her face because she couldn't stop. She'd lost control.

I smiled, because if there were some joke in what he'd said, I didn't want to seem stupid. But then I replayed what he'd said in my mind: "Well, archaeology. That's really a different subject." It didn't seem funny to me, so I stopped smiling.

Stephen raised the camera and lunged forward on one leg, as though he were going to sword-fight. I jumped, thinking something was wrong, but he was only photographing that hummingbird.

"He's a photographer for the *Clarion*," Ivy reminded me. She'd regained control and now looked rather solemn. I noticed the subject of my career had been dropped for his.

"He has to photograph basketball games, wrestling matches, and mother-daughter teas, but he's really interested in wildlife, especially birds."

"Oh," I said, "well, then, I hope he likes to fly." It just slipped out. I couldn't help it. I smiled to show it was all in good fun.

Ivy snorted again. "Oh, Staaaarr," she wailed.

Stephen fiddled with the lens of his camera. Maybe he didn't know how to use it, or maybe he wanted to ignore the fact that I'd one-upped him.

"Well, I've got to go," I sighed, digging my hands into the front pockets of my jeans.

"Wait a second," Ivy said, pulling me a few feet away. She turned so that her back was to him, and then barely containing herself, began to gush, "Isn't he something? Can you believe I'm here with him?"

I looked at her to see if she were serious. She was. "He's kinda . . ."

"*Smart*, yeah, he is," she said, rolling her eyes. "Listen, Starr. Would it be all right if we went to the movie tomorrow instead? 'Cause I'm not going to make it in time."

"What?" I slowly pulled my hands from my pockets. I was stunned. "Not go to the movie? Why?"

She glanced at Stephen and shrugged. "Well . . . like I said . . ."

I lifted my hand to shield my eyes from the sun, but I really wanted to cover my face. This hurt feeling was rising up inside me, and I didn't want Ivy to see it.

"What are you doing here anyway?" she asked me.

"I'm looking for Julie. Why did you come here with *him?* I thought he was just bringing your notebook over."

"He asked me to go for a walk. Boy, was I surprised. I'm really nervous. Am I acting all right?" She took my hand and squeezed it.

*Acting* sounds about right, I thought. But I didn't say that. I just looked at her and shrugged and tried to figure out what was going on. I just didn't get it.

"I can't go to a movie tomorrow," I said.

"How about Monday? I can go Monday. Can you go Monday?"

"Calm *down,* Ivy. Yes, I can go Monday. *I* can go Monday, can you go Monday?" I sighed, feeling a little exhausted by all her energy.

"You're making fun."

"Well, you're acting so goofy. What's wrong with you?"

"Nothing." She sniffed, pointing her nose in the air.

"Well, I've got to go find Julie. I guess I'll just have to see you on Monday." I looked at her, hoping she'd change her mind, but she was barely paying attention to me. I turned to say good-bye to the psycho dresser, but his face was hidden behind the camera. I smiled, just in case he took a picture, and drifted away.

# CHAPTER 7

I was afraid that by the time I reached *Pinus sylvestris* in "Southwetern Astralia" Julie would either be crying or gone. She was neither. She was sitting on a tree stump, with her head down, twisting the stem of a small yellow flower between two fingers.

I'm not sure why, but when someone has hurt my feelings, I want to turn around and do the same thing to someone else. It wasn't right, and I knew it, but I considered leaving her there awhile by herself, to let her think I wasn't coming. I was standing behind a big fern tree. I watched her for a few minutes, twirling the flower around and around and around, and I soon became bored. You can only do that sort of thing for so long. I stepped out from the shadow of the tree into the sunlight and marched toward her.

"You know, Julie," I called to her, "you have a lot of nerve dragging me over here like this. I told you I was going to the movies. What's the matter with you?"

"Nothing. Didn't you think the note was funny?" She smiled, like she was trying it on for size.

I came right up to her, putting my face up close to hers. "No, I didn't. I threw it in the toilet. Come on, get up. I'm tired of chasing you around. I have a life, you know, Julie. I had *plans* for today." *Had*, I thought. That about says it.

She held up the flower. "Look. It's pretty, isn't it?"

"Hmph," I grunted, heading for the paved pathway. She had no choice but to follow or be left behind, so she hopped off the tree stump and began to trail along behind me, the soles of her sandals clopping like small horse hooves.

"You're going too fast for me, Starr! Wait up!"

I surged forward, not slowing a bit. "You wanted to hike, so we're going on a hike. I'm sorry you were stupid enough to wear sandals. Everyone knows you don't wear sandals when you go hiking. Everyone but you, Julie. You better wise up. Start doing some thinking."

*Clop clop. Clop clop.*

The fact that she wore sandals to go hiking just enraged me. It was like wearing little pumps to play tennis, or high heels to bowl in. I would've known better by the time I was seven. She was nine. I heard her sniffling behind me, and that only made me madder.

*Sniffle sniffle. Clop clop. Sniffle sniffle. Clop clop.*

"You know, you're not a baby anymore."

"I know I'm not a baby! I just forgot to change shoes! Is that a big deal? Wait, Starr, wait!"

"Mom's *really* mad at you for coming here alone," I yelled over my shoulder. A blast of cold water struck my face as I hurried between the arcs of two sprinklers set in the ground alongside the path.

"I didn't come here alone. I came with you. I just got

here first. Besides, nobody was home when I left. So I couldn't get permission."

I stopped and turned, and she ran right into me, her head butting my chest. *Thunk.* "Ouch!" I cried. "Nobody's home up *here*," I said, rapping the top of her pale blond head with the knuckles of my right hand. "*I* don't even come here alone very often."

She pulled away from me with a fierce look in her eye. "You're in such a bad mood! I'm sorry I took your sweatshirt. I was only kidding around, and you're so serious about everything!"

"You irritate me, and you do it on purpose. Now tighten those straps on your sandals! We're not going any farther until you do. I'm not going to carry you home after you fall on your face."

She knelt on one knee, mumbling. "I know why you're in such a bad mood."

I stood glaring down at her, hands on my hips, swatting a gnat humming in my ear. "I'm not in a bad mood."

"Sure. *Sure* you're not in a bad mood. And we're *really* in Australia too."

If I hit her I would regret it later. "Hurry up. How can it take you so long to fix your straps?"

"You're not perfect either."

"Nobody said I was."

"You're in a bad mood because Ivy has a boyfriend."

In my mind I saw myself give her a good chop on the shoulder, and then a good shove. It wasn't so much what she said as that smug look on her face. I knew the psycho dresser was no more Ivy's boyfriend than Albert Einstein was mine. True, she gave up going to the movies with me to be with him, and I was mad. But that no more made him her boyfriend than going to the zoo made you a lion tamer.

"You're being silly, and you don't know what you're talking about."

She stood up with a defiant look in her eye. "Yes, I do. I saw them together, here in the park."

"Really?" I said indignantly. "What're you doing following her around? I don't think she would much like the idea of being followed around by a nosy little kid."

"I wasn't—"

"C'mon. I'm wasting my whole day." I whirled and began to march down the path through Western Australia. Above us, a little scrap of pearly gray fog crawled across the sky from the west. Sun fog. Sun fog. You couldn't turn your back on the sky for a second. Or your best friend either.

"You can make new friends," she called eagerly, sliding along behind me.

"Why would I need new friends?" I called back to her. "You're the one in need of friends, baby sister!" Ha, I thought. What a little chump she is!

"Well, maybe . . ."

"Don't see this as an opportunity. We're not going to become best friends. Not now or ever. You're my *sister*, and don't forget it!" I was going at a good clip along the path, and her sandals were now scraping along the ground behind me.

"You never know. . . ."

"Well, *I* know, Julie, so forget it, and just keep walking."

"*Carin*," she sniped.

Here the path forked, and I took a left turn down a long string of narrow wooden steps set into the hillside. The steps led down to a creek. I told her to be careful, as I hopped onto some long, flat rocks to get across the creek. The rocks were wet, and I nearly slipped myself.

"*Prunella vulgaris,*" said Julie, coming up close behind me.

"What?" I said irritably, turning to glance at her.

"*Prunella vulgaris.*" She laughed rather weakly; I guess she was hoping I'd laugh along with her. I didn't. I just said, "Mmm."

"You wish I was dead, don't you?"

"Julie, for gosh sakes!" I leaped over the last rock to the creek bank. "That's an awful thing to say."

"Oh, right! Now you're even lying to me." She was sniffling again.

"I'm not lying," I insisted. "Why would I wish you were dead?" I stopped and turned to face her.

"Well, it's just a feeling." She stuck out her lower lip.

"Well, I don't know where it came from, but it's wrong. I don't wish you were dead, I wish you were . . . different. I wish you were . . . less . . . more . . ."

"Your age."

I looked at her and shrugged. "Actually, I don't wish that either."

"Oh." Her eyes grew misty. She sniffed.

"Let's go. All right?"

She nodded.

I walked a little slower, so she could keep up. We soon came into a large clearing, where a lot of people were gathering up blankets as the sun slipped into a swirl of fog.

"Oh, good," Julie gasped as we approached a row of benches. "Let's rest for a while, okay?" She hobbled ahead of me, then plopped herself down on the bench, pretending to gasp for air.

"I don't have time, Julie. You can rest at home. C'mon, get up. We're hiking, after all, just like you wanted."

"You're lucky," she whined, banging her heel on the bench leg. "You're going to the movies. I wish I could go."

I didn't say anything. Then I thought, well, yes, I *am* going to the movies. I would go alone, and treat myself to a big bag of popcorn. Nobody would know that I went alone. Therefore I wouldn't have to answer questions about why Ivy didn't go, and no one would think to tell me to take my time when I wasn't in a hurry in the first place.

"This wasn't much fun," Julie whimpered, now limping along behind me.

"No, it wasn't," I agreed. "So next time I won't come chasing after you. Remember that." Even as I said it, I knew it wasn't true. I would come chasing after her again, because I'd never leave her in the park alone. I'd die if anything bad happened to her, even though she nearly annoyed me to death.

I had a miserable time at the movies. The popcorn was cold, the movie was stupid, and as I was leaving the theater I saw Ivy and Stephen coming in. They didn't see me. I was thankful for that.

As I hurried to slip away without being seen, I felt as I had in the third grade, when Kim Ippolito knocked the head off my snowman, then went to build one with Ashlee Hunt.

This was betrayal, an act of war, a call to action.

# CHAPTER 8

But what? What could I do to get back at her? My father had just taken a pan of brownies from the oven and set it on the kitchen counter. Normally this would make me very, very happy. I sat at the kitchen table reading the daily comics. This was also something I usually enjoyed, but today they didn't seem that funny. I couldn't keep my mind on them anyway. I kept seeing Ivy say she couldn't go to the movies, and I kept seeing her walk into the theater with Stephen.

I mean, I *knew* Ivy. She wouldn't do something like that, but there it was. She had.

It was now about five o'clock on a Saturday that I now considered to be a total waste, a zero.

"Wanna brownie?" asked my dad as he slid a knife along the edges of the pan. "These are Super Cosmic Brownies. I used to make them for your mom when we were dating."

"Okay. Where is she?"

"Out in the yard, playing with the new weed killer. Mmm. I don't know why chocolate makes you feel better, but it does."

I hadn't told him anything was wrong, so I wasn't sure if he was talking about him feeling bad about something or me. As I did not want him to know anything was bothering me, I said, "Uh-huh," and went on twisting the four corners of a yellow paper napkin into little pointy daggers.

I was thinking about how much I hated her and how mean she was. I would never trust her again. I would call off her birthday dinner, and when I told my parents why, they wouldn't blame me. I could say something right now if I wanted to.

My father was whistling. Therefore, it did not seem like precisely the right moment.

I turned a page. The Emporium was having a big sale. I skimmed the ad, hoping for a bargain on swimsuits. I would not walk to school with her, nor would I sit with her at lunch, much less share what was in my brown bag. In my mind, I watched her face crumple as I strolled past her table to join Lindy Wicker, whom Ivy intensely disliked. But then I didn't care for Lindy much either.

I tossed the paper aside and got up to get a glass of milk.

"How'd your day go?" My dad rolled the sleeves of his shirt up to his elbows, as though he were about to perform a delicate operation, then lifted a large square brownie out of the pan with a spatula. "You look a little glum."

"Oh, you know," I sighed.

"No, I don't. Tell me." He carried the brownie gingerly across the room and set it down on my mangled yellow napkin. "These Super Cosmic Brownies are made from scratch."

"It was a weird day," I said simply, setting my milk on the table and sitting down.

"Oh, I've had weird days."

"Have you?" I replied flatly, tearing off a chunk of the brownie and popping it into my mouth.

"Certainly. I'm a weird person, so I have a lot of weird days."

It was true. He not only taught foreign languages at a nearby high school, he also read Latin for fun. He often has said it's too bad more people don't know Latin, that it's not really a dead language. He hopes someday to write a series of books, something like *Latin for Lovers, Latin for Young Lovers,* and so on. We decided to help him out with other ideas and started a list on the refrigerator:

*Best Latin for Baby-sitters* (me)
*Latin for Farmers* (Dad)
*Popular Rodeo Latin* (Mom)
*Best Backpacking Latin* (me)
*Lullabies in Latin* (Julie)
*Best Latin Phrases for Your Trip to Scandinavia* (Ivy)
*Latin Quotes for Cabbies* (Aunt Sharon)
*Manhattan Latin—A Pocket Guide* (Mom)
*Power Latin for Pitchers* (Uncle Kevin)
*Beach Blanket Latin—How to Impress Your Friends* (me)
*Why Teach Your Grandmother Latin?* (Grandma Fran)
*Little Latin Lulus—Surprise Your First-Grade Teacher* (Mom)
*Best Latin Names for Your Pets* (Julie)

"*Julie!*" he suddenly bellowed, "*C'mon 'n' get it!*" He flopped back across the kitchen to the counter in his rubber thongs. Birds of a feather, I thought. He had brown hair now, but I'd seen pictures of him as a kid, when it was that same cheesy yellow as Julie's.

"You and Julie went hiking?"

I nodded.

"Then you went to the movies, didn't you?" He pulled a chair out and sat down across the table. "Mmm, good. I wonder why they call them 'brownies.' After all, we don't call plain white cake 'whities,' or yellow cake 'yellowees.'"

"I don't know, Dad. You're the language teacher."

"*Julie!*" my dad called again. Then, hunching over his Super Cosmic Brownie, he asked, "What's this about Ivy's new boyfriend? Julie said she saw them in the park."

I flattened a crumb on the napkin with my thumb, then another. "I don't know, Dad. As far as I know, Ivy doesn't have a boyfriend. Some guy returned a notebook she lost. I could be wrong, though. Julie does seem to know everything."

"Aha. I see. Well, I'm glad Ivy doesn't have a boyfriend. Because if she were old enough to have a boyfriend, you could be old enough to have a boyfriend. But that would mean *I'd* have to be old enough for you to have a boyfriend, and I'm not. Someday, when we're all a little older, we can talk about boyfriends, okay? Isn't this good? Isn't this the best brownie you've ever had?"

"Mmm-mmm, just about." I stuffed the last of the brownie into my mouth and wiped my mouth with the napkin. Then I crumpled my napkin into a ball and tossed it toward the trash can.

"These are getting cold, aren't they? *Julie!*"

"Dad, just leave her."

"Why, what's wrong?"

"Nothing. You know. Sometimes she just likes to . . . to sulk." But it was too late. She was flopping down the hallway, headed our way.

"Oh," he said, with a puzzled frown. "Yes, she does. And why might she be sulking today?"

I knew exactly how her face would look, all pulled out of shape like taffy. As I got up to get a refill from the refrigerator, she peered around the corner.

"Hey, babe," said my dad.

She smiled begrudgingly back and then started limping across the kitchen, a baggy sweatshirt hanging down to her knees.

"What's wrong with your foot?" he asked.

"Blisters," said Julie.

"Oh, too much hiking, I guess," he added.

"No, too *fast*," she replied.

"No, wrong *shoes*," I said crossly.

My dad got up and flopped toward the brownie pan. "I know." He chopped at the air with the spatula to emphasize his point. "I know! Let's all stay home tonight, all of us together. It's April, it's spring! We can order a pizza and rent a movie, or play some music and sing! Wheeeeeeen thuuuu moon hits your eye like a big pizza pie . . ."

Julie wouldn't look at me. I started to get mad again. It was her idea to go hiking, and we'd gone.

"I'm going to read tonight," I said. "Alone."

My father glanced at Julie and then at me.

"I'll have pizza, Daddy," she said.

"I'll have pizza, Daddy," I mimicked in a whisper. I set the glass on the counter, banging it down hard by accident as he sliced a brownie for Julie. He glanced up at me in surprise, then paused to make it a warning.

"Starr, this is Julie. Julie, this is Starr. I hope you'll get to know and like one another, since you're going to be related for the rest of your lives." Then he went on humming. "When the moon hits your eye like a big pizza pie . . ."

"Carin," Julie corrected.

"Oh, that's right," he said. "C-C-C-C-C-arin. My C-C-C-Carin."

She giggled.

"When the moon hits . . ." Now they were singing and flopping around the kitchen together. Genetics. It was everything.

I fled to the living room, thinking maybe I would listen to some better music on the stereo. I knelt beside the stack of old tapes next to the cabinet, pulled one out, and slipped it into the tape deck. It was by the Moody Blues. Then I settled back onto the sofa and lowered the headphones over my ears.

The music was heavy and somber, and suited me fine just then. My best friend had betrayed me. As the Moody Blues wailed on about the agony of lost love, I wondered how come. I stared at my feet, wiggling my toes in my dirty white socks, and that made me think about him, the psycho dresser, and why Ivy would want to go to the movies with somebody who talked like the host of a *National Geographic* special, instead of with me.

I drew my knees to my chest, wrapping my arms around them. I won't do it, I thought. I won't go gaga for some weird, boring guy like Stephen, and I don't understand why Ivy did.

I stuck my cold hands under my butt, trying to warm them. I knew that my mom was in from the yard because I could hear the three of them singing, even with the headphones on. Normally I would join them and try to forget my worries, but I didn't want to. I felt like being alone.

I shut my eyes, but soon I heard this voice inside my head whispering, "Don't go out with boys, don't go out with boys, don't go out with boys." I opened my eyes, afraid I'd suddenly gone "round the bend," as my Aunt Sharon would say.

It was my dad, kneeling beside me. He'd lifted one of the earphones and was speaking into my ear. "Don't go out with boys."

"Why not?" I asked him.

"Because, I know what we're like."

I smiled.

"I ordered your favorite pizza."

"Thank you, Daddy . . . I mean Dad."

Julie was lurking in the doorway. "Thank you, Daddy," she silently mimicked.

I chose to ignore her, preserving my dignity. Besides, my father was whispering again in my ear.

"Tomorrow I'll make some pinkies. . . ."

I lifted the headphones. "Some what?"

"Raspberry muffins. Now, for an appetizer, how about some soupee? It's just from a can."

"I think I'll wait for the pizza." I put the headphones back on and closed my eyes. After a little while the pizza came. I was just about to get up and head for the kitchen when I heard loud noises.

I yanked the headphones off, thinking Julie was messing with the stereo. But there she was, standing by the kitchen door, with an awful look on her face.

"They're fighting," she whispered.

"Who?"

"Mom and *Dad.*"

"No, they're not," I hissed back, because they hardly ever did, and when they did, it frightened me and I hated it. But it was a stupid thing to say, because I could hear them:

"What do you *think* I mean?"

"You don't have to say it like *that.*"

"Why not, it's the *truth.*"

"Dad dropped the pizza," whispered Julie. "It's on the kitchen floor."

"The *whole* pizza?"

She nodded.

"Oh, no."

She looked worried and scared as she edged toward me on the sofa. I could've been a better sister right then, talked to her a little, told her it wasn't the end of the world. But it seemed too hard. It felt like moving a mountain, and I just couldn't do it.

"Just go on down to your room. They'll figure it out," I said flatly. She nodded and began to tiptoe down the hallway. In a minute I did the same thing myself.

We did have dinner that night. Canned soup and French bread. It was like one of those silent meals you eat in a monastery. *Tick tick tick* went the clock on the wall above the kitchen table.

I went to bed early, hoping the next day would somehow be better for everyone. When my mom came in to say good night, she asked me if I was all right. I said I was fine, just tired, hard practice. I fluttered my eyes to show I was just sleepy. I could have been more truthful. I could have said I felt like the princess in "The Princess and the Pea," and the pea was Ivy's betrayal. It seemed like a small thing and felt like a big thing. Maybe I was just being too sensitive.

My mom or my dad used to read to me before bed every night when I was a little kid. I could've used a bedtime story then, but when you're twelve going on thirteen you don't ask for things like that.

Before I fell asleep I sensed another pea under the mattress, but I didn't know what it was. Actually, it felt more like a grain of sand than a pea. I'd forgotten to do something, but what?

# CHAPTER 9

As soon as I opened my eyes the next morning I remembered Estella's tortillas. Dimwit, I said to myself. Goofball. I groaned and rolled over, then forced myself to get up because I wanted to take care of my mistake right away, give the new day a chance. As I slipped into a pair of jeans and a sweatshirt, I listened for voices, but the house was quiet. Too quiet.

My parents were seated at opposite ends of the kitchen table. "Morning," I said, immediately sensing they were separated by more than a plate of raspberry muffins.

"Good morning," they replied crisply, each rattling a section of the Sunday paper. No, it had not yet blown over.

I noticed, as I hurried up the stairwell to Estella's apartment with the bag of tortillas, that it seemed unusually quiet here also. No barking dogs, no barking birds, no loud TVs, no nothing. I knocked three times and slipped the key into the lock. As I came through the door she raised her head and tried to smile, but she looked terrible.

I thought maybe she was mad. "I'm sorry," I said, holding up the bag of tortillas as I tried to catch my breath. "I meant to bring them yesterday. I just forgot."

Then I saw that she'd been crying. "Estella," I said, setting the bag of tortillas down on the end table, "What's wrong?"

"Isabel," she said, dabbing at a single tear as it crawled down her cheek.

I glanced at Isabel's cage. It was empty. "Where is she?" I said, refusing to let my eyes wander around the room, lest she was lying dead somewhere.

Then she told me how Isabel had been bad all day Saturday, how she'd barked and demanded one sandwich after another all through the baseball game until finally Estella locked her in her cage to teach her a lesson. Estella dabbed at her cheek as though she'd reached the end of the story.

I waited. Something inside me was saying, You don't want to know the rest of this story; but it was too late.

"After a little while I felt bad. She's very quiet and I know she sulking, so I go and open the door. I say, 'Now you stay quiet, Izzie, so I can hear the end of the game in peace. The Giants are down by a run.' She says nothing. Just stands there with her toes curled over the swing. No flip-flops, no nothing. Then the grocery boy comes, and she fly out the door. *Brrrrrmmmm.*" She fluttered her hand through the air like a bird. "He left downstairs door open. . . . A little mistake and she's gone."

I cleared my throat, turning red. "The grocery boy," I repeated. "He should've . . ." I couldn't finish the sentence. It was too embarrassing trying to pretend it wasn't my fault.

"It was my fault," she said, "I should have pay attention."

I gazed at her sad, brown face, then turned to look out the window. The noisy city was quiet for a change. Just the wind whistling around the side of the building and a foghorn sounding mournful somewhere out in the ocean. A streetcar clanged past, nearly empty, and it was a bit how I suddenly felt inside. "I'm sure we'll find her," I said, trying to feel hopeful instead.

"She's lost, or somebody took her."

"Oh, no, she'll come back, Estella. She loves you." I needed to believe this, but even as I said it, I was filled with doubt. I heard another distant foghorn, sounding like sorrow itself, and I thought of Isabel out there somewhere, maybe lost, flying low over a dark, frothy sea, crying, "Make me a sandwich, make me a sandwich!" I hoped Estella could not read my mind.

We opened a window in case Isabel wanted to fly back in. Then I brought Estella a warm Pepsi and turned on the TV, but I could tell she was only looking at it, not really watching. I also heated some soup and lined the plate with crackers. She looked at the tray of food with a gray, sour face. Sour and sorrowful. She did not look well.

The smell of sea air was gradually replacing Jungle Gardenia in the apartment. In fact, as the room grew colder I began to shiver, and so before I left I brought her a shawl from the bedroom and laid it around her shoulders.

"You are very kind," she said, sniffing twice. "And don't look so sad. Maybe she's happy." Then, amazingly, she smiled, picked up her spoon, and began to eat.

I knew she did this so I wouldn't feel bad. She was the kind one, not me.

The wind billowed the curtains and rattled the empty birdcage as I slipped out of the apartment. I felt really bad. Maybe I hadn't made the worst mistake in the world, but I still felt guilty, selfish, and stupid. It was a good thing I couldn't see ahead to the rest of the day.

# CHAPTER 10

I had only one thought on my mind as I stood uncertainly in front of Estella's building, chewing on a fingernail. I couldn't stand the thought of her sitting up there all alone, and I intended to do something about it. As I did not have to be home until noon, I had some time to do some immediate searching. But where? First I looked down the left side of the street, then down the right, then back down the left and back down the right, wondering where in the world a parrot would go. I hadn't a clue, only a wild hope that I'd suddenly hear that raspy little voice asking for a sandwich. As that was not likely, I began combing the neighborhood. I got a lot of suspicious glances as I ran up and down the streets calling her name, but I didn't care. It was not a time to be self-conscious.

I did get tired, however. After about twenty minutes, I stopped to catch my breath at a light that had just turned green. I was sweating, and I mopped my face with the sleeve of my sweatshirt. I needed something to drink but I didn't want to spend any money, so I decided to cut over to the park and head for a drinking fountain.

That was where I saw them, crossing the street at Seventh and Irving. Ivy and Stephen. They weren't that far ahead of me, so I stopped. My face suddenly felt hot and my hands got cold. I couldn't believe she was with him again, the psycho dresser, and I couldn't believe I'd nearly run into them.

I stood at the corner, my arms folded around my chest, my heart beating wildly inside it. I would let them get a safe distance ahead of me, then go get a drink and come back.

The light at the corner turned green again. I licked my lips and slowly crossed the street. Staying a safe distance back, I ducked behind a tree once and a dumpster twice, just like in the movies. What could I say if they saw me, that I was out looking for a lost bird?

I stopped at another traffic light at Lincoln, shifting my feet as I waited for it to change. One day, years ago, Ivy and I stood at this very corner and stuck out our tongues at passing cars, just to see what would happen. Finally a woman stopped her car, got out, and started to chase us, screaming that we were stupid brats. I guess we were.

I quickened my pace as they slipped between the big eucalyptus trees straddling the edge of the park. Suddenly I had this strange and awful realization. I didn't want to lose them. I wanted to see where they were going and what they were up to. Don't be silly, I said to myself. You don't want a repeat of yesterday. You don't want to see Ivy dance around on her toes again, like somebody you don't know. You don't want to talk to the psycho dresser about dinosaurs and genetics. You've got to find Isabel and you have to do it now.

I took off after them. Nutcake, I said. Goofball. Two

skateboarders with Walkmans flew past me, then two girls on Rollerblades. Like on most Sundays, the park was crowded. Everyone seemed to be in a twosome but me, even the old man walking his spaniel. Maybe I could talk Mom and Dad into getting a dog, so I would have someone to be with. Also, a dog wouldn't do this to me. A dog wouldn't say it would go with you to the movies and go off with its boyfriend instead. But even dogs run away, I thought glumly. Maybe they shrink and then join that mysterious band of little fog doggies roaming the sky. Hang on to your pet, mister.

The sky was so clear. No fog in sight. I passed a small circle of men playing conga drums. One with no teeth grinned and winked. Maybe I would get a big German shepherd. I put my head down and hurried along, but that was the wrong thing to do. I'd lost them.

I blinked nervously, scanning the area. There they were, crossing JFK Drive, heading away from the arboretum. Where were they going? And how could I be doing this, trailing them like a golden retriever, a bloodhound?

I stayed well behind them as they cut across a long grassy field, because there was nothing for me to hide behind if they turned around. I thought surely they would turn toward the arboretum after passing the pond but they didn't. They cut over to the road, heading farther into the park. I was puzzled.

Now that they were up on the winding sidewalk I could get closer. They hesitated before a wooden bench but went on. I wondered what you talk about with someone you don't know very well.

I remembered I'd once had a long talk with a boy I also didn't know very well. His name was Armand Joseph, and we were on a science project together. We talked about fossils, our teachers, and Shana Barampour's Valentine's party, to which he was not invited. Armand moved the next year, not because he wasn't invited to Shana's party. It had to do with a parent's job. Maybe we would've become friends, gone on into the seventh and eighth grades talking about petrified wood.

They ambled onto a paved path climbing to Stern Lake, and I was close enough to hear them laughing. Ivy and I had been to Stern Lake too, once by ourselves when we ate a box of Oreo cookies, and once with our sixth-grade teacher, Mr. Boles, on a nature walk in the fall. We walked around the lake collecting leaves and had green tea and almond cookies in the Japanese Tea Garden.

I followed them past bushes exploding with many beautiful flowers, now down a dirt path angling close to the water. He took a picture of a big, ugly black goose. Then he took her photograph—no, several—in front of a tree by the water. Some assignment this is, I thought. Some wildlife photographer. Maybe just wild. I bet that's it. I bet she's in a lot more danger than she knows.

I was surprised she stood so close to the water. Two steps back and she'd be in. We don't know him. He could be a lunatic and push her right in, though it's not deep right there. I imagine that happening anyway, and I rush forward to save her, after I lay him out cold with a punch to his nose. We're best friends again. She decides to put off dating for a few more years, say ten or eleven.

Actually, the time we came here alone she had to help pull me out of the mud and I ruined a new pair of sneakers. But I didn't think she was remembering that right now. She took his picture. He leaned against the tree like Mr. Cool, Mr. Big Man, Mr. Come-and-Get-Me.

They were holding hands. Just ahead of them were several rowboats and paddleboats tied to a small wooden pier. Stephen wandered up to the window of the rental shack. He walked back to Ivy. She laughed. I could tell, even though her back was turned to me. She twirled around on her sneakers with her hands behind her back.

Then an amazing thing happened. She followed him to the boat and climbed in. She crawled onto the front seat, in the bow, and he settled himself into the stern. He pushed off the pier with an oar and started rowing.

Maybe I had the wrong couple. Maybe I was too far behind them and ended up following these look-alikes. The real Ivy would never get into a boat. I knew this as well as I know the back of my hand.

My mouth had fallen open. I watched from behind the bush as they glided toward the middle of the lake. He dipped and pulled, dipped and pulled, taking her away. She leaned back, smiling. She looked like she was fifteen, or seventeen, but it really was Ivy.

I had tried to get her into a canoe and couldn't. Her mother couldn't get her into a boat. Her brother, whom she idolized, couldn't get her into a boat. But this boy with bad socks and a camera had. This must be falling in love.

That was where I left them, or they left me, she leaning back comfortably in the bow as though she were born there, her hand trailing the water. I imagined throwing a big heavy fossil at Stephen's head.

Instead I turned away, swiping at a bee buzzing close to my ear. As I headed back down the path around the lake I had a little talk with Ivy. I said, Someday you'll be sorry. He'll dump you, and you'll know how this feels. You see if he'll go to the dog show with you. You see if he'll try out new dances with you in front of your parents' long bedroom mirror. See if he'll help you make deep-dish pizza. No, he'll just sit there and stuff his face.

Out of energy, I sank to the ground beside the water. Yanking a fistful of grass from the ground, I tossed it aside, then another. Just wait and see. Someday you'll be sorry. You'll need me, and I'll be nowhere around. I'll be off having fun without you. I'll be a famous archaeologist or geologist. I'll have more friends than I know what to do with. They'll be movie stars and athletes and presidents and oh, yes, maybe a famous photographer. I'll sail down the Amazon and descend into the deepest ocean and discover new fish and they'll be named after me. Starr . . . fish. No, I sighed, that was already taken.

I wanted a DoveBar. No, two. There is no way anyone can eat two DoveBars right in a row, but I wanted to try.

As I watched the ducks dunking for food, I picked up a twig and twirled it between two fingers, dislodging its last brittle leaf. I tossed the twig into the pond. Just as it was being carried away by a gentle current, somebody behind me screamed bloody murder.

*aaaaaaah! Starrrrr!"*

I leaped to my feet and whirled. It was *Julie*, running in circles, chased by the big black goose. *"Honk honk honk,"* it cried, nipping at the seat of her pants.

What in the world? I thought. Then I ran toward her, clapping my hands and shouting, *"Hey, shoo, scat!"* The goose took a last nip at her butt, then took off in an all-out waddle toward the water. *"Honk . . . honk . . . honk . . ."*

I grabbed Julie by the shoulders. "Julie! Are you all right?"

Her face crumpled as she burst into tears. "It *attacked* me. It chased me! It tried to bite me and wouldn't stop!"

"I believe you're okay," I said calmly. She pulled me toward her and buried her face in my chest, sobbing. "All right, all right," I sighed. I didn't feel much like consoling anyone but myself right then, but I tried, patting her shoulder and brushing her hair from her face.

"Look, it wouldn't really hurt you or they wouldn't be able to keep them in the park," I said. "I mean, they don't have teeth. They don't really bite."

"It . . . it wanted my Goo Goo." She extended and unclenched her hand, which was smeared with smashed-up Goo Goo.

"Oh," I said with a grimace. "Well, see, you and the goose have something in common. She can't be so bad then, can she?"

She rubbed her butt. "Now it's ruined."

"Don't worry, it'll grow back."

"I mean the Goo Goo."

"Oh. Yeah, that is ruined. But I bet you've got another one to take its place. Don't you?"

She smiled and nodded.

"Turn around. See, no marks even. Does it hurt?"

"A little." She peeled a sliver of Goo Goo Supreme from her open hand. "Want some?"

I wrinkled my nose in revulsion. She was a case, a real case, this sister of mine. Should I be nice or should I scold her? Then I wondered . . .

"Julie, what are you doing here?"

"What?"

"I said what're you doing here by yourself? *Again.* You know the rules. Stop stalling."

She shrugged. "I just came to the park."

I narrowed my eyes and studied her face. I was suspicious. "Mmm, mmm. You just came to the park for what?"

"I came to . . . feed the ducks. Yeah."

I looked around for a bag, or something that might contain bread crumbs. "To feed them what?" I put my hands on my hips, feeling more and more suspicious and slightly annoyed.

She shrugged again, staring sullenly at the ground and

then at her Goo Goo. "It's ruined." She threw a worried glance over her shoulder. The big goose was back and closing in, waddling in a wide circle around us.

"You're got thirty more of those things at home. Everybody in the park could have a Goo Goo." Then another thought occurred to me. I folded my arms across my chest, anticipating indignation. "Julie, you weren't by any chance following me, were you?"

"What?" she asked, turning up to me a bewildered and innocent face.

"C'mon, out with it."

"I saw you. Running down the street. Then you stopped. I saw Ivy and—"

"You snoop! How dare you!" I was suddenly furious and shook a fist in her face to show it. So much for the nice, nurturing sister. I tore a chunk of Goo Goo from her hand and threw it to the goose, which grabbed it and ran. Julie let out a yelp. If she'd had a double-decker turkey sandwich with bacon and cheese and all the trimmings or a hamburger and french fries, I would've thrown that to the goose too.

"There! You got what you deserve, you little brat. You big baby! That'll teach you to spy on me! Don't you ever do that again!"

She backed away from me, looking scared. "You were doing it too!" she cried. "You were spying and I saw you!"

I turned red with embarrassment and anger. Then, I'm not sure how, but it happened. I swung my arm back—and smacked her.

She fell backward onto the ground, cowering, as I glowered down at her, my chest heaving with rage. Then, as her eyes brimmed with tears, I looked at her in horror. The whole left side of her face was now a bright crimson red. My hand dropped to my side, and I thought, I didn't do that. Before I could think of anything to say, she scrambled to her feet and took off running.

My right hand still stung as I took off after her, yelling. "I can't go *anywhere*. I can't do *anything* and there you *are!*"

What if she runs away, I thought, and I never see her again? But it didn't take me long to catch up to her. I grabbed a handful of her shirt from behind and hung on. She tried to pull away and then turned and tried to kick me, but I still hung on, until we tumbled together to the ground.

"You never want to be with me! *Never never!*" She pounded the ground with her hand and the heel of her shoe, as the goose did a quick side step in the opposite direction.

I didn't know what she was talking about, and I was still furious. "Oh, you baby. Baby baby baby," I fumed.

She burst into tears. The gulls cried with her and the pigeons cooed. I was still mad but I was also scared. Her face was still red. What had I done?

I finally let her wrestle out of my grip, as she whimpered and sniffed and wiped her nose with her hand. Then I sat back on my own hands. Underneath me they couldn't do any harm.

Meanwhile, word had spread, and we were soon surrounded by an army of ducks and geese and pigeons all hoping for Goo Goo.

"You hate me. You never do anything with me."

I sighed. "How can you say that? We're *always* together. I don't hate you. How can I hate you?" I said, trying to be generous. "You're my sister. I just hate when you act like this. No wonder you don't have any friends."

"It's the only reason we're ever together. Because we're sisters."

"Oh, cool the routine, Julie. Look, I'm sorry I hit you, but you shouldn't have followed me. See what happens when you go where you're not invited? You get into trouble. . . ." I didn't finish the sentence.

I let out another exasperated sigh and looked around us. A teenage girl with long black hair sat nearby, drawing ducks on a sketch pad. An old man was reading poetry out loud to another old man. A woman handed out pieces of bread to some little children to feed the birds. The ducks and pigeons rushed toward them. It was spring vacation.

"Well, look," I said, "we're not in demand anymore." Fickle little creatures, birds, I thought. Fickle as friends could be.

Julie wiped her tear-smeared face with her sleeve.

"I guess they all want some," I said, hoping we could forget what had happened. "Like what's Goo Goo for the goose is Goo Goo for the gander."

She didn't laugh. Maybe she didn't get it. I turned to look out across the little lake. I didn't see them, but I knew they were out there somewhere having a great time, and I was stranded on shore with my little sister and her smashed-up Goo Goo.

I turned to look at Julie, who was eyeing me warily. As we slowly made our way out of the park, she licking Goo

Goo from the palm of her hand, I remembered Ivy's saying she wanted something exciting to happen, and wondered, miserably, if a boyfriend was what she'd meant from the start.

# CHAPTER 12

We were heading up Highway 101 across the long span of the Golden Gate Bridge on Sunday afternoon, and we were late. The play up at Mount Tamalpais started at 1:00 P.M., and it was 12:35.

"Please don't drive like a maniac, Stuart," said my mother. "It's not worth it."

"I'm not. How could I drive fast? Look at this traffic."

"Well, you're tailgating. It's not worth it."

My father sighed. We all sighed. He slowed a bit and glanced at the dashboard clock. "We're not going to make it."

"Then we'll do something else," my mother replied, her tone of voice putting the matter to rest.

I was in the backseat with Julie, who was practically crawling up her side of the car to stay away from me. Every so often I stole a sideways glance at her face, to see if I'd left a mark. I hadn't. That made me feel only a little better.

"I guess we could go somewhere else for a picnic," mumbled my dad without enthusiasm. "We've got all this food. We could go to the park."

"I don't *want* to go to the park!" I cried.

My mother turned her head, frowning. "Why?"

"I . . . I'm *sick* of the park."

"Huh," remarked Julie.

"Let's sing," said my dad. "It'll pass the time."

"Okay," I said, then started in on "One Hundred Bottles of Beer on the Wall," which drew a stern glance from my mother.

"See," she said to my dad, turning toward the front again, "she does take after your aunt Alma."

"Nah. That's from your side. Aunt Alma would never sing about alcoholic beverages." He hit the turn signal and headed for the exit.

It's a family joke. When Julie and I are behaving well, they're both eager to claim genetic responsibility. When we're not, they'd each prefer we took after the other's made-up Aunt Alma.

We had now come to a dead stop, stalled in a line of cars as far as I could see.

"You bring the Frisbee, Christine?"

My mother shrugged. "No. Why would I do that? I thought we were going to see *Othello*."

"It's in the garage," I said.

"Figures," mumbled Julie.

I had an almost unbearable urge to jump out the window, figuring a broken leg would be better than the atmosphere inside the car.

It was hot as blazes, even with the car windows down. We had to eat some of our food because we were getting so crabby and hungry. We forgot napkins, so I wouldn't touch the chicken, just the rice and salad. To pass the time my parents told us the story of *Othello*:

MOM: This play's about a very trustworthy general, Othello, his beautiful wife, Desdemona, and the villain, Iago.

JULIE: Eeahgo? How do you spell that?

MOM: I-a-g-o. Iago.

DAD: Iago's mad and jealous because Othello picked someone else, a guy named Cassio, to be his lieutenant. So Iago makes up this plan to deceive Othello into thinking Cassio has become romantically involved with Desdemona.

JULIE: How do you spell Desdemona?

ME: Julie, what does it matter? Just listen!

DAD: D-e-s-d-e-m-o-n-a.

MOM: Othello is a trusting sort of fellow—pass the chicken, honey—and falls for Iago's tricks. He becomes so jealous he tells Iago to kill Cassio.

JULIE: Why doesn't Oh Fellow kill him himself?

MOM: Because generals don't do the dirty work. They hire somebody else.

ME: It's Othello, Julie. O-t-h-e-l-l-o.

DAD: Then, hmm, let's see. Iago tricks another soldier into stabbing Cassio, but Cassio is only wounded and kills the soldier himself. Othello finds out that Iago tricked him, but first he kills his wife Desdemona out of jealousy.

JULIE: How?

ME: With weed killer.

MOM: She does remind me of your aunt Alma.

DAD: Aunt Alma would never say that.

MOM: She had a sharp tongue. You were afraid of her.

JULIE: What's a sharp tongue?

DAD: Little biting remarks.

JULIE: Oh. (*She looked at me.*)

MOM: Sometimes they hurt people's feelings. (*I was very sorry I'd tried to be funny.*)

JULIE: Have you ever been jealous?

DAD: Sure, lots of times.

JULIE: Were you ever jealous of Mom?

DAD: Before we were married, she had lots of boyfriends.

JULIE: Mom, were you ever jealous of Dad?

MOM: Oh, I suppose this one time.

DAD: You were? When?

MOM: We're getting off the track. After Othello discovers that Desdemona really was faithful to him, he wounds Iago, then falls upon his own sword and dies. Cassio becomes the general.

DAD: What one time?

MOM: It's about how all along you can think you're doing the right thing, and it's really the wrong thing. That's what makes it a tragedy. It's when bad things happen to good people.

DAD: Jealousy can make a mess of things, no matter who you are.

JULIE: I'll say. What'd we bring for dessert?

I wasn't thinking about food. I was thinking about all these people killing each other. It made my problems seem smaller. Maybe that was why people went to these things.

We missed the first act, and had to sit way in the back, the four of us scrunched together on a narrow wooden pew. Julie would not sit next to me. I wasn't surprised, but I began to feel strange because she'd never acted like this before. No matter what I did, she never stayed mad for long, until then.

Maybe the play should've made me feel like a million dollars, knowing I wasn't the only one who had trouble getting along with people. But it didn't. I couldn't seem to get what had happened off my mind. Every so often I'd have to lean forward, pretending to tie my shoe or look at someone. I would glance at her face. I kept wanting to make sure I hadn't left a mark. Then I'd sit back and try to concentrate on the play, but after a while I'd be sure I *had* left a mark—I could actually see it in my mind—and I'd lean forward to retie my shoe.

Back in the car Julie made an announcement. "I'm going to be an actress." I knew this was information for my parents, not me. Normally I would have snorted a smart reply, like, "*Going* to be an actress!" But I didn't.

"It's a hard job," I said, "but I bet you could do it."

She didn't answer, and I didn't try again, just turned to stare at my sad-looking reflection in the window.

The fog was rolling and tumbling its way through the Golden Gate as we came through. It was awesome.

"What a sight," declared my mother. "I'll never take this for granted."

My dad took her hand. "I'll never take you for granted either." She smiled.

"*Forson et haec olim meminisse irivabit,*" he added. "Someday it shall be pleasing to recall these things."

They were done fighting. I looked at Julie, hoping this would be an inspiration. No, it would not.

When we arrived at home and stepped out of the car, I looked at Julie and winced. A big red imprint about the size of my hand covered one cheek. I was about to make a heartfelt apology, but she slammed the door and ran inside, leaving me standing beside the car like a dope. Then I realized the mark was on the wrong cheek. It was red because she'd leaned against the window, but it didn't much matter. It didn't change things.

# CHAPTER 13

I heard the phone ring, my mother marching down the hallway, and then the rap on my door.

"For you, Starr."

I got up out of bed and staggered groggily down the hallway.

"Morning, honey. I think it's Fizz."

I picked up the receiver, hoping she was wrong. Fizz was a girl I didn't like very much. She lived across the street and went to a private school. Usually I turned her down when she invited me to do things, because she often acted immature for her age. Sometimes this got on my nerves or embarrassed me.

We said hi, and then she said that she and her older cousin were taking her twin brothers to the zoo after lunch and asked me to come along.

I thought for a minute, remembering it was Monday, and Ivy and I had plans for a movie. Then I said yes. I figured I might need new friends. There was this long pause. I knew Fizz was surprised—and then I could hear her jumping around. Calm down, I thought, annoyed by such needy behavior. It's just the zoo.

Julie was slurping a bowl of cereal at the table. Normally this would annoy the heck out of me too. But as I hung up the phone I turned and told her I was going to the zoo. She looked at me and went on reading her cereal box.

"Do you want to go with us?"

She shook her head.

I stood there for a few seconds, not knowing what to say because she'd never turned me down before.

"Why not?" I finally asked. "You love the zoo."

"I'm going to work on my poems."

"We're not going until after lunch. You'd have plenty of time."

She went on reading. I was now less interesting than a box of Cap'n Crunch. "Well, work on your poems," I said, still standing by the phone. I didn't dare come closer for fear I'd be wearing the bowl of cereal on my head. "Who knows? Maybe if you keep at it you'll get invited to that party. Have you written any new ones?"

Now she looked at me. "Yes, I have. It goes like this:

> "Starr Starr
> Please go far.
> Away."

"Look, Julie, er . . . Carin, I said I was—" Then the phone rang and I had to answer it.

"Hi, Starr. It's me."

It was Ivy. "Hi," I said briskly.

"Can you come over?"

Come over, I thought. Oh sure. She sounded so casual, like nothing had happened.

"Starr, are you there? What's the matter?"

"Yeah, I'm here," I said, yanking the zipper on my sweatshirt up and down, up and down, "but I can't come over. I'm going to the zoo."

"You are? With who?"

I took a deep breath. It was pretty clear she hadn't remembered our plans for a movie. But now I didn't want to go anyway. "With Fizz."

"With Fizz? I didn't know you did things with her."

"We're going with her cousin, who's older."

"Oh, I hope it's fun."

"So do I."

"Can't you stop by for a minute, just to see something?"

"I don't think so," I said. "What is it?"

"Come over and I'll show you."

I watched the second hand on the kitchen clock jerking the seconds away.

"Oh, come on. Just for a few minutes."

I felt myself begin to weaken, partly out of curiosity, partly because I just missed her. But I wasn't ready to say yes. I wanted her to beg me.

"I don't know. I've got a lot to do before I go out. . . ."

"Aw, really?"

"I guess I could stop by for a few minutes, after I eat."

"Oh, good. Oh, goody. What're you having?"

I looked at Julie slurping the cereal. "A Goo Goo Supreme."

"A *what?*"

She started laughing, and I laughed a little with her. Suddenly I felt hopeful, like maybe after a while things could go back to normal. Maybe she'd come to her senses and drop him. Maybe she'd apologize and we'd have a great week after all. People make mistakes. You have to forgive them. Now I was sorry I'd said yes to Fizz. *Fizz.* I didn't want to go to the zoo with *Fizz.*

Before I could hang up the phone I had to twirl seven times to the left to untangle myself from the telephone cord. Julie was still at the table. I took the box of Sunrise Granola from the cabinet and poured some into a bowl. I got a spoon and sat down at the table. I said, "Could you pass me the milk?" She slid the carton a few inches toward me, then took her bowl to the sink and walked away.

My mind was a muddle of thoughts and feelings as I sailed down Fifth Street on my bicycle. Perhaps I shouldn't have jumped when she called me. Perhaps I should've played harder to get. I had no idea what she wanted to show me. Should I mention the movie or not?

The sun was breaking through the little fog doggies full force, and I was grateful. I hated staring at the tigers and bears on a cold, windy day.

Her mom let me in. I headed for Ivy's room at the end of the hall, like I'd done a hundred times before. Right away, I thought something was strange. Ivy was curled up in a chair by the window, a pair of black binoculars hanging from her neck. "Hi," she smiled. "C'mon in."

"Hi. I am in." I took a few awkward steps across the

room and sat down at the edge of her bed. Then I tossed her a Goo Goo. I could've thrown it a lot harder, because I was still mad, but if she was going to apologize I didn't want to ruin it.

"What's this?"

"It's a breakfast Goo Goo. It's like a granola bar, only it's chocolate, marshmallow, pecans, caramel . . . something like that. Julie ordered about a hundred pounds from some place in Tennessee. I'm trying to get rid of them one by one." I forced myself to smile.

"Breakfast Goo Goo," she said with amazement. "I don't think I can eat this."

"Why not?"

"I can't eat something called a Goo Goo. Besides, I'm still fat."

"Then go on a diet."

She glanced at me with surprise.

"You don't need to lose weight," I added. "And don't forget dinner tomorrow either."

"I won't. What's up with you?"

"Nothing. Diets are stupid."

"I just want to look good in shorts for the summer."

"You look fine in shorts," I said, and shrugged. "Here, toss me the Goo Goo. I'll eat it. So what's the big secret? Why'd you want me to come over?"

"It's not a big secret, Starr. It's just something I wanted to show you. Come over here and look outside, out the window."

I pulled myself up and then casually slouched my way toward the window. "Yeah?" I said, evaluating my first taste of Goo Goo. It wasn't that bad. As I took another bite, I gazed down into the small, square, fenced-in yard bordered by neat rows of tulips, irises, and other spring flowers. "Okay. I'm looking," I said, smacking my lips. "Now what?"

"Don't you see it?"

"No, what? Can't you give me some kind of hint?"

"Look harder—at the tree! Now do you see?"

I saw a square brown bird thing hanging from the eucalyptus tree. That was all. "The bird thing?" I said. "What is it, a . . . a feeder?"

"Yep."

I saw this very satisfied smile on her face, and I felt like laughing. "What's so special about that?"

"I just put it up. It'll attract all kinds of birds."

"Yeah? So? Is *that* what you wanted to show me?" I looked at the birdhouse. I looked at the binoculars, studied her face, and noticed behind her a ratty old bird's nest sitting on her dresser. I'm pretty good at math, and things began to add up.

I said, "Ivy, you hate birds, remember? Ever since we saw that scary movie when all the birds attacked the people in that little town."

"Well, maybe I outgrew that," she said thoughtfully.

"Since *Friday?*" I said. "Oh, *c'mon.*" I counted out the days on my fingers. "One, two, three, four."

"I can like birds if I want."

"Well," I said briskly, "just what species are you trying to attract?"

"Oh, I don't know, anything really," she blurted with enthusiasm. "I don't know that much about them yet, but I want to learn."

"You're talking about birds?"

"Uh-huh."

"What's that saying? 'A bird in the hand is worth . . .'?"

"Two in the bush."

I said, "Or is it a *boy* in the hand is worth . . . ?"

She leaned forward and punched me lightly on the shoulder, laughing. "Oh, Starr!"

This girl was happy, and a little sarcasm wasn't going to stop her. She swung around to face the window and held up the binoculars. "These belonged to my dad. . . . I found them in the attic, along with the bird feeder. Mom said they're mine if I want them. You can see every little detail. It's great. Have a look." She lifted them up over her head and passed them to me.

"I see what you mean." I was just pretending to look at the bird. I was looking but not seeing. I could see every detail of this little brown bird, but what did I care? I was thinking. She brought me here to see *this*? She hung a bird feeder in her yard to get the psycho dresser to *like* her? Was I supposed to get excited? Was I supposed to be happy about this? I didn't know what to say.

"How long have you been sitting here?" I asked her.

"All morning. Stephen told me what kind of birdseed to buy."

"Wow. What a guy."

"He's really neat, don't you think?"

"I think maybe you're moving a little fast. You just met him. I'm surprised your mom is letting you see him so much."

"She thinks he's nice, and I didn't just meet him. He was in my study hall, remember?"

"That's beside the point, isn't it?" Now I lowered the binoculars and looked at her. "I mean, you're only thirteen!"

"Gee, Starr. You sound like an old woman. Oh, look! Something with a reddish blue head!"

"It's Mrs. Myberg," I said, lifting the binoculars again. "What's she doing in your birdhouse?" Mrs. Myberg was our music teacher. Her hair was always changing color, depending on the angle of light. I don't know why I was trying to be funny, but Ivy laughed. And it made me feel better, at least for the time being.

I handed the binoculars back and sat down on her bed. "Remember that wildlife class we took together at camp last summer? That poor counselor, what was her name, always trying to get us to tell the difference between a nuthatch and a wren."

"Oh, yeah. It was Cheesy or Chesty or something."

"*Chesty!*" I burst out laughing. "I don't think so!"

"I wish I had a camera. This bird's so cute!"

*This bird's so cute!* I mimicked to myself. When did she start to *sound* like that? Yuk. Then I heard this little voice from the past. It was Ivy. We were playing with our Barbie dolls. *This one's so cute!* I heard her say. I could see her brushing the doll's brown hair in her lap. I wished it was then, and we were down there in her yard playing with our dolls under that tree and not up here now looking down at a birdhouse she bought because she wanted some guy to like her.

She hadn't yet asked anything about me, not what I'd done for three days or anything else. Usually I'd blurt it all out, but now I held back. She might say, "Oh, really?" and go on looking at that finch or whatever it was. I didn't think I could take it.

It was quiet for a minute. Then she said, "Stephen says birds are direct descendants of some species of dinosaur. I forget which ones."

"We talked about that on Saturday," I mumbled through a mouthful of Goo Goo. "Don't you remember? Genetics and all that."

"Oh, that's right. Well, he also said that archaeologists have discovered the remains of some small dinosaurs with wings."

"I know," I said, looking right at her. "Remember? I'm interested in that stuff too."

"Oh, that's right." She smiled a little sheepishly.

We grew quiet again. We just sat looking out the window for a while, until I said, "I wish it was summer already. I can't wait to go back to camp, you know? We'll be with the Rubies this year and get to do some outpost camping." I glanced at her out of the corner of my eye. She'd picked up a book and was flipping through it.

"I just can't wait, you know?" I repeated.

"I'm not sure . . . well . . . I'm not sure I'm going." She stopped flipping the pages and gave me a long, serious look.

I swallowed hard. "Why?" I said hoarsely. "Don't tell me it has something to do with *Stephen?* You hardly know him. Don't tell me you're going to give up your whole summer because of him?"

"I'm not giving it up. I just want . . . a different kind of summer. I don't want to make the lanyards again." She tossed the book on the bed with an air of finality.

I wished she'd been acting goofy when she said that. But she sounded like the old Ivy, the one I'd stayed up nearly all night with, talking about how far away the stars were, about God and our fear of latrines.

"I don't either. I'm sick of lanyards too. Take horseback riding and acting or dancing and woodworking. Take swimming and canoeing and get over your fear of the water. Take—"

"Starr. I'm going to Yosemite for a week with my mother and brother. And Stephen was telling me about this coed camp run by the Sierra Club."

"Coed? What do you mean?"

"Boys and girls together. You know, like college."

"So you're skipping high school. Wow."

"You're so goofy. We're in the same camp, but not in the same tent or cabin. My mom wants to think about it."

"I'll be she does. You share the same bathroom?"

"I don't know. I doubt it." She sighed. "Starr, what do you really think of him?"

"I don't know," I said flatly.

"You must have some idea."

"Well, I don't know about *him*. I only met him once. But if you really want to know what I think, I'll tell you. You know when I saw you with him on Saturday?"

"Yeah?"

"Now don't take this wrong. But you were acting pretty stupid."

Her hand flew to her mouth. "I was not!"

"Yeah, you were," I insisted. "The way you were laughing and bouncing around. It wasn't natural. It wasn't like you." I popped the last piece of Goo Goo into my mouth, even though I was slightly nauseated. After all, I'd just had breakfast.

"It was too!"

"No, it wasn't."

"How would *you* know what's natural?"

I didn't like the look on her face. "What do you mean?"

"You've never had a boyfriend. You don't know how you'd act!" She picked up the book again and rifled absently through it.

I felt the heat mount in my neck and face. This was because I knew she was right, but I didn't admit that. Instead I said, "I would be myself. I know I would." This was nearly a lie, and my face remained red.

"I think I know what's going on," she hissed, her mouth contorted in an ugly snarl.

"Oh? What?"

"I think you're jealous because I have a boyfriend and you don't."

"I'm not jealous of your boyfriend."

"Yes, you are. And get the crumbs off my bed."

"No, I'm not." There were only a few crumbs, and I ignored them.

"Then *what?*"

I felt my eyes go misty and I swallowed, turning my face toward the window. How could I say what I was feeling? Then, because I didn't know what else to do, I just blurted it out. "I feel . . . left out. That's what's going on. That's why I'm mad." Then, embarrassed, I lowered my head as a single tear spilled onto the crease in my thumb.

"Starr," she murmured, "are you *crying?*"

"No, not really." I quickly dabbed my eyes. "It's . . . just . . . you're my best friend and I haven't seen you in three days and we had all these plans. . . ."

"But you're here now, aren't you?"

"Yeah, for fifteen minutes," I sighed. "You had to squeeze me in to your busy schedule."

"You're the one going to the zoo. Not me."

*"I wouldn't be, if you didn't spend all your time with the psycho dresser!"* I lifted my head now and glared.

"The *what*? The *who*?"

"I saw you at the movies, Ivy! I saw you!" She was surprised by this—I could tell by the way she sort of folded in on herself, dipping her head and hugging her arms to her chest.

"Hmph. It wasn't my idea. It was his!"

"As if you don't have a mind of your own. Look, Ivy, I hate to tell you this"—I sniffed and tried to sneak another wipe at my eyes—"but maybe I'd better."

"What? What are you going to say? Just tell me!"

"Well," I said, moistening my lips. "The guy's . . . he's not that great a catch. He's really kind of a jerk, don't you think?"

She leaped off the bed and began to stomp back and forth across her bedroom. "Oh, nice! That's really nice, Starr! My first boyfriend, and you call him a jerk. Some friend you turned out to be!"

*I* turned out to be, I thought miserably. What a laugh. I shook my head in disgust but kept an eye on her. She still had the book in her hand, and I was ready to duck. "You asked me what I thought, didn't you? So now I'm telling you."

"Okay, well, thanks so much for your opinion," she snapped, turning to glower from the other side of the bed. "And it *is* an opinion. Don't you have to go now? Aren't you going somewhere with *Fizz?*"

I stood up slowly, seething mad, so mad I could hardly breathe. "You're *changing.*"

I hardly intended this as a compliment, but she said, "I know, and I'm glad." She said it fiercely, glaring at me with her fists on her hips.

I glowered back, then shot across the room and out the door.

I rode my bicycle through the park like a maniac. I was flying. Everything I passed was a blur. If Isabel was around I never would have seen her. Oh, if only I'd never left the safety of my bed!

After a while I calmed down and did some serious searching. Then I went over to Estella's to give her the bad news. She didn't seem surprised; she was still sad, but at least she had the TV on.

I didn't feel at all like going to the zoo and at first had to force myself to laugh along with Fizz and her cousin Sudi. The cousin was also immature, so it must have been "genetic." We spent most of the afternoon there because Fizz had to stop and imitate every animal, and every now and then I got into it too. It was a relief to act stupid and not worry about anything. I was embarrassed, however, during her baboon imitation, because it was too real. People stopped to stare and applaud. Their babies cried and had to be comforted. Even the baboons seemed surprised.

\* \* \*

By the time I was supposed to go shopping with my mom that night I felt pretty glum and awfully discouraged. I certainly didn't feel like shopping for Ivy's birthday, but I definitely didn't want to mention our fight to my mother. Telling it would make it more real.

Because it was raining, we ended up at the only large indoor mall in San Francisco. I bought Ivy a small blue journal that zippered shut. My mother bought her three mystery books.

On the way home Mother asked me if anything was wrong.

"Not really," I said, gazing out the window on my side of the car.

"You're not having a good vacation, are you?" she asked.

"Not really," I replied, licking my lips, trying to keep a steady hold on my voice. I guess she figured I didn't want to talk about it, because that was all she said. When I got home I wrapped the new journal in Ivy's ratty old balloon scarf. I sat looking at it for a while. Maybe if I gave it back to her, she'd wear it again, and turn magically back into herself, the old Ivy, whom I missed very much.

CHAPTER 14

My dad and I spent a lot of time baking that cake. "Whipping up" was more like it. A lot of my fury went into it. It had four layers, filled with three different flavors—raspberry, chocolate whipped cream, and semisweet chocolate fudge. Then we frosted the whole thing with the chocolate whipped cream.

The first time I set the dining room table I did it all wrong, placing the knives and forks on the wrong side of the plates. I also forgot the place mats. It was around six, and Ivy was supposed to come over around 6:30. The truth was, I didn't care if I ever saw her again. I didn't know *how* I was going to pretend to *like* her in front of my parents. I couldn't imagine smiling or saying anything nice. I couldn't imagine talking to her at all. "Happy Birthday, you snot," I would say. "Some good friend you turned out to be."

My dad was slicing tomatoes in the kitchen. My mother was dicing chicken for a Chinese stir fry. Julie was watching TV. Ivy doesn't deserve this, I thought as I went hunting for candles, rifling through drawers in the kitchen. She certainly wouldn't do this for *me*. I found a box of candles, counted out thirteen, and placed them on the kitchen counter beside the cake. Somebody else could put them on.

At 6:20 the doorbell rang. She's *early*, I thought with alarm and surprise, and knocked into a chair on my way to answer the door. But it was somebody registering voters door to door. I flopped down on the floor in front of the TV. Julie lay sprawled on the sofa.

"Are you hungry?" I said.

"Mmm mmm."

"What're you watching? Oh, *Swamp Thing*, I've seen it. Don't worry, in the end somebody blows it up before it kills everybody." She still wasn't talking to me.

There was a knock and I got up again, this time moseying my way across the room. Well, she has come, I thought, ready to force myself to smile. You can be civil for one evening, I told myself. After all, it is her birthday. But I would not forget what she'd said and what she'd done. "I think you're jealous because I have a boyfriend and you don't!" she'd shouted. I got myself all worked up again replaying it in my mind, so it was a good thing it was Irene Chew from across the street, telling us her father-in-law died. (I was not glad her father-in-law died.)

My mom talked to her for a while, went back to the kitchen, and reappeared in the living room a few minutes later.

"Dinner's about ready," she said with a concerned look on her face. "You told her six-thirty, right?"

I nodded.

"Then I'll keep it warm."

I stared at the TV, seething inside. She had a lot of nerve being late, when my parents were going to all this trouble. Let's eat without her, I wanted to say, but I didn't. Instead I turned back to the TV as the Swamp Thing emerged, full of muck from the swamp.

"She's not coming," said Julie, scowling. "Can't say that I blame her."

"Yes, she is. She's just late." Then I scanned Julie's face with suspicion, wondering if she knew something I didn't know. She will come, I thought. She wouldn't do that to me.

"You should call her. See what's holding her up," said my mom from the door that led to the kitchen. "Your dad's picking garbanzo beans from the salad."

"Let him," I felt like saying, because I was feeling worse with every passing second. "I don't want to call her," I blurted, still staring at the TV screen. "Let's go ahead without her. She can eat when she gets here."

"Are you sure? It is her birthday," she pleaded. "Don't you think we should wait?"

"I can't remember what she said," I mumbled, turning red. "I think she told me she'd be late and we should go ahead without her." I didn't look at my mom. Surely she could see I was lying, but I just couldn't stand for them to see how hurt I was. *I* was the daughter who had it together. *I* was the one who had friends.

"Oh?" replied my mother. "I guess you forgot to tell us." She hesitated for a few seconds, waiting.

I shrugged and turned back to *Swamp Thing*. Soon I heard the drone of my parents' voices in the kitchen.

Maybe they were saying I was a misfit like Julie, something they'd suspected all along. By 7:15 I just gave up. I knew she wasn't coming. Though I wasn't interested in eating, I forced myself to get up. "Let's eat," I mumbled. "I don't care if it's her birthday."

"Told you," muttered Julie under her breath.

My mother, conveying her concern through quick, puzzled glances, removed two platters and a loaf of bread from the oven and set them on hot pads on the table. My father tossed the salad minus garbanzo beans with a homemade raspberry vinaigrette dressing. "How's the movie?" he asked cheerily. "Are you hungry? Doesn't this smell good?"

The Chocolate Heart Attack, now adorned with thirteen pink and blue candles, sat smack in the middle of the table.

"It's Tuesday already," said my dad as we scuffed our chairs against the floor and sat down. "Isn't the week going by fast?"

Not fast enough, I thought gloomily as I placed very small helpings of rice and stir fry on my plate and passed the bowls to my father.

"It's not like her," said my mom. "I hope she's all right. I hope nothing happened. I still think we should call her. What if . . ."

"This is really good, Mom," I said, trying to swallow. "Yum."

"Can we turn the movie back on?" blurted Julie. "Where's Ivy? Is she with her boyfriend? You can't really blame her." She was sitting right across the table and still wouldn't look at me.

"That was such a weird movie," I said, hoping to

change the subject. "Do you know how the swamp thing kills everyone? It has bad breath from being in that swamp for a million years." I snorted and looked at my dad, hoping it would get him laughing. He smiled and said, "That's funny, honey," in such a tender way, I nearly choked on my food.

But I kept on trying. "Swamp breath," I said through a mouthful. "It's the kiss of death."

"How very disgusting," said Julie.

I couldn't seem to eat any more, so I pushed a snow pea around the edge of my plate, trying to remember what I'd said that would make Ivy hate me so much.

"No, you can't really blame her," sighed Julie.

"Julie," hushed my mother.

I lowered my head and put down my fork because I couldn't face them anymore and couldn't swallow another thing. I just kept poking the snow pea.

"Starr," murmured my mother.

"Yes," I said, looking up. She looked very sad. I felt bad because she'd gone to so much trouble to fix a nice dinner.

"Honey, you should wipe the front of your shirt."

I looked down in amazement at a long brown dribble staining the front of my favorite white shirt. To keep my lip from trembling, I bit down hard and dug my thumbnail into the side of my finger. A slow panic was rising up inside me, and I wanted to stop it.

"Oh," I replied. Then, leaning forward to dip the end of my napkin into a pitcher of water, I knocked over my glass of milk.

I heard Julie snicker and out of the corner of my eye saw

her try to stifle it with a hand on her mouth. She'd never laughed at me like that before, so I was surprised that it really hurt me.

I kept my head down; my face was ablaze with embarrassment. Then an odd thing happened. I heard myself think, You can't really blame her. As the milk shot across the table, I glanced up at Julie. Suddenly I could imagine this long stream of hurt feelings, and they weren't mine, they were hers.

I knew I should go get a sponge, but I just sat there like a lump until my mom got up for me. Then I pushed my chair from the table and headed down the hallway to my room. I closed the door behind me and flung myself onto my bed.

As I lay there grasping my pillow, I thought about all the times Julie needed me and how I refused her. I thought about all the times she'd asked me to do things and how I said no. I heard her snicker again in my mind and wondered if I'd turned her into a mean and selfish person, just like me. It seemed that things couldn't get much worse. Up until then I'd had a best friend I could count on and a sister who liked me. You took things like that for granted, and then they were gone.

I looked at the fog rolling in, and my eyes began to fill with tears. Suddenly I could hear this voice, my voice, saying, "You big baby . . . baby baby baby . . ." I stuffed my face into the pillow, but still I could hear it. "Oh you baby . . ."

After a little while my mother came in. She wanted to make sure I was okay, and I said I was. I just didn't want a discussion. After she left I sat there gazing out at the sky. It was pinkish gray from the streetlights and mostly drenched in fog, except where a sliver of moon showed through. I stared at the fog very hard, trying to see if I could make out the face of a fog doggy, like I'd always looked for the man in the moon.

When I was little, seeing the man in the moon used to be like magic. I would have to stare at it awhile before I could make out a nose or a mouth. But I always found him. Then, when I was eleven, my parents got me a telescope. I never forgot the first time I looked through it. I didn't see a nose or mouth, of course, only a lot of crags and craters. I felt very grown-up seeing the moon that way. It was exciting. I wanted to go there.

You would think that after that it might be hard to see the man in the moon ever again. After all, I now knew what I was looking at. But with my powerful imagination it was not very hard. Besides, he was like a big friend hanging up there in the sky. I did not want to lose him.

I did feel a little foolish, looking for a fog doggy at my age. But there was only a sliver of moon, and I needed a friend right then.

The fog floated low overhead. Just before dusk turned to dark I saw one. It looked like, of all things, a little Chihuahua straining against its collar. I blew my nose, feeling silly but grateful.

I was closing the curtain when a small slip of paper appeared under my door. I picked it up. It was a note from Julie.

*Dear Starr:*

*Would you like some chalklate cake? I culd get it for you.*

*Love,*
*Julie*

Normally I would hang out in my room for a while, make her think I was not too interested in spending time with her. I didn't do that this time because it would have been a lie, and I'm not good at lying. I got into my pajamas and tiptoed across the hall to her room. Her door was open and her light was out. I was still sniffling as I got into bed and slipped underneath the covers. She was facing the wall, her long willowy legs drawn up toward her stomach. I could hear her breathing, and when she swallowed it was so quiet I could hear that too.

As I slipped my arm around her waist, I could smell the baby shampoo in her hair and feel the baby softness of her skin. She took my hand and pulled it to her chest. I used my other hand to wipe my nose with a balled-up tissue.

"Big baby," she whispered.

"Oh shut up," I said, and pinched her lightly.

"No cake?"

"No, but thanks for offering."

"You're welcome.

> *"Jake Jake*
> *Bake me a cake.*
> *Roland Roland*
> *Let's go bowlin'.*

*Ashlee Ashlee*
*Take out the trashy."*

"I hope you get invited," I said, yawning.
"Me too."
I drifted off in the middle of the "lullaby," right after

*"Karen Karen*
*What you wearin'?"*

# CHAPTER 15

I was making a sandwich. It was about noon the next day. My dad had taken Julie to the dentist, so I was home alone. As I spread peanut butter across one slice of whole wheat bread and blueberry jam across the other, I worried about Isabel. I'd gone looking again that morning and still hadn't found her.

I slapped the two halves of the sandwich together and cut it in half. Then I poured myself a glass of milk and sat down at the table. The house was absolutely quiet. Usually I enjoyed having it all to myself. But the truth was, I was a little lonely.

After I ate the sandwich I put my plate in the sink. I had a craving for something sweet and searched the cabinets for cookies. I couldn't find any, and was about to go hunting for my mother's newest hiding place for candy, when I remembered the Chocolate Heart Attack. It sat at the end of the counter, covered in Saran Wrap, the candles in a pile beside it.

I removed the Saran Wrap and grabbed a plate from the

cabinet. Nobody had touched the cake. I guess they were trying to be nice, or waiting for me. I didn't want it to go to waste, so I took a knife from the drawer and made a neat incision. Then I transferred a large wedge of the cake onto the plate and poured myself another half glass of milk.

I sat down at the kitchen table. Happy birthday, Ivy, I said to myself, because it was today, Wednesday, that was really her birthday. Then I sank the fork into the cake, careful to get a nice portion of chocolate fudge, and took a big bite. It was very good and very sweet, sweet as my sister.

*Do you want a piece of chalklate cake? I culd get it for you.*

It was not right that my parents and I had worked so hard for nothing. Ivy should've come by or called, angry or not. I wiped my mouth with my napkin, and then, either because I had a good imagination or a good memory, I saw her sitting on that rock back on Friday, telling me what she really wanted for her birthday.

Doesn't matter, I thought grimly. Right is right, and I didn't think I could forgive her.

*Do you want a piece of chalklate cake? I culd get it for you.*

I had that piece gone in no time, but I still felt sad and lonely. Then I remembered what my dad said about chocolate making you feel better. So I got up and helped myself to another. After all, I'd made the darn cake, and didn't want to waste it.

As I sat down again, I tried to imagine the cake Ivy's mother might have made. Maybe it was made with tofu, or maybe it had seaweed frosting. Poor Ivy. Still, right is right, I thought, sighing, again heading straight for the chocolate fudge. I relished every bite, and when I was done, I still wasn't full. Well, this is lunch, isn't it? I thought in defense of myself. Then I wasn't sure what happened. Maybe it was genetics again. Maybe it was my Grandma Anna waving a hand in my face, warning me not to enjoy myself. I put down my fork, picked it up and licked it clean, and put it down again. Then I shoved my chair back, strode over to the Chocolate Heart Attack, and sliced another huge piece. This piece I placed on a paper plate under a sheet of Saran Wrap. Ivy's presents were sitting on the table, and I scooped them up too. Then I went to the front door and opened it.

"Oh!" I exclaimed, nearly dropping the presents. It was Ivy.

"My mom made me," she said, shrugging, gazing at the doormat.

"Oh!" I exclaimed again, because I was really flustered and hadn't had time to plan what to say. "Well, um . . ." Later I would wonder how long she'd been standing there, and if she'd planned on ringing the bell.

"I'm supposed to apologize for not calling, or coming over, so I apologize because my mother wanted me to. But I'm still mad."

"So am I." We stood there eyeing each other, until it got too awkward and uncomfortable, and I said, "Well, you wanna come in or just go?"

She shrugged again, careful not to look at me. "I don't know."

"Well, come in then," I said. So she followed me back into the kitchen. I put her piece of cake on the table and the presents on the counter.

Normally we would've been yapping away by now, but

we were acting like strangers. "Are you having a nice birthday?" I said. It seemed like a safe thing to say.

"Oh, all right, I guess. My mother's making me another cake, I think she called this one a banana surprise. They're *always* surprises. Anyhow, I saw a new kind of granola on the counter and I hope it's not going in it."

"It probably is. You want a piece of this cake, then, don't you?"

"Yeah." She went to pull out a chair and stopped. "Are you having some too?"

I didn't want her to eat cake alone on her birthday, so I said, "Sure," and went to the counter to slice another piece of Chocolate Heart Attack for myself. Then I poured us each a glass of milk, and we sat down together. It's hard to look someone you're mad at right in the eye, and I was still mad. I picked up my fork, spread the napkin neatly across my lap. She did exactly the same thing, and we looked at each other.

"When you opened the door," said Ivy, "were you on your way to my house?"

Once again, I thought about lying, because I didn't want it to look like I was the one who ought to make up. And I thought about saying something smart-alecky, like, "No, I was on my way to a meeting in London."

"As a matter of fact, I was," I replied.

"Oh," she replied, blushing. "Mmm. Did your dad make this?"

"My dad and I made it together," I said, "but I picked out the recipe. You know, because it's your birthday." Now I did look at her, and I saw that she was trying hard to look like none of this mattered. But it did. I put down my fork and sighed. "You should've come over, Ivy. You should've at least called me."

She nodded, her eyes growing misty. "I was so mad at you for everything you said. I just couldn't come over. But it wasn't right. I'm sorry."

"I'm sorry too. I'm sorry I hurt your feelings and called Stephen a jerk. He seems . . . interesting."

"My mom thinks he's too old for me. I told her we went to the movies, and that ticked her off. I can't see him anymore. By the time I'm old enough to go out with him, he'll be engaged." She blew her nose into a napkin. "I really like him. I do. Sort of. He's not a jerk, Starr."

I could've jumped for joy, but I didn't even smile. "That's too bad, Ivy. Did he give you a birthday present?"

"He gave me a picture he took of me sitting in a boat at Stern Lake. Can you believe I did that? I don't even look scared—I think I was too excited—so I've put it up in my room. I've got to get over this stupid fear of water. It's so embarrassing."

Someday I'd tell her how I followed her and Stephen to Stern Lake, and what happened with me and Julie. But it didn't seem like the right moment. "You'd be surprised by what people are afraid of."

"Yeah? Like what?" she asked. "Mmm. This is the best cake I've ever had."

"Chihuahuas, for example." It was the first thing that popped into my mind.

"*What?*" she said, laughing. "Oh, come on."

"Oh, it's a known fact. Chihuahuaphobia. They remind

people of rats. I also heard about this one guy who was so afraid of postage stamps, he never paid his bills and had to declare bankruptcy. Nobody else in his family was afraid of postage stamps, so genetics is only part of it, particularly in advanced forms of life. Take a look at the turkey vulture."

"*What* turkey vulture?"

"Exactly my point. They're becoming extinct." I smiled.

"And so will you if you keep this up."

"Sorry." I set my fork down and flattened my hand against my stomach. I suddenly did not feel very well.

"Did you really think he was a jerk?"

"No," I said, stalling for time. "I think he's got potential, but he's only fifteen. Very young for the male species."

"I wish I hadn't hung that bird thing. The birds start screeching outside my window really early."

"You hate birds, Ivy. Remember? I'll help you take it down." I was making a conscious effort not to reach over and flick a crumb from the corner of her mouth. But I figured these things have a way of disappearing on their own, unlike life's larger problems.

Like too much cake. I had to lie down.

Even though I spent a lot of time looking, we never found Isabel. I only went to camp for one week that summer so I'd have money to buy Estella another bird, which pleased her very much. I knew I couldn't bring Isabel back, but I spent several hours standing in front of Waddell's cage, trying to teach him to talk.

"Make me a sandwich," I'd say.

"Hello, darlin'."

"C'mon, Waddell, say 'Make me a sandwich.'"

"Hello, darlin'."

"I'm hungry. Make me a sandwich, Waddell."

"Hello, darlin'."

Waddell had a mind of his own, but it ran on one track. Once in a while I brought Julie along to Estella's. She was shy at first and pretended to like baseball so Estella would like her. But after a while she gave that up. I was never sure if it was the caffeine in all the Pepsi or Estella's attention that sent Julie spinning around her living room in a whirl of cartwheels and backbends.

Julie did not get invited to Rachel's party. But she had a new friend, Jacklyn, whom she sometimes brought to Estella's. So Estella had plenty of company.

Ivy and I did go to camp together. We made up stories about the psycho dresser and got in trouble for causing some of the other girls to have nightmares. She took beginning swimming, and I took it with her, even though I knew how to swim.